I0718811

NOBEL CREST

AN AUTOMATON NOVEL

Imogene Nix

Cover Art by Dexpress Covers

Editing by Hot Tree Editing

EBook ISBN 978-1-922369-51-2

Paperback ISBN 978-1-922369-52-9

Dear Diary,

It seems Francesca Hemingswood-Whitmore is as determined as ever to live her life in an unconventional yet honest manner.

Amaryllis, my dearest sister, asked her to visit now that Dawn has arrived. Such a pretty little girl she is, with the cutest nose and shining eyes. So quiet and dainty.

In the last few years, I know Francesca's spent many days at the house known as Nobel Crest as a guest of Adam Nobel—at least until he passed. In many ways, it seemed she preferred his company to ours, yet there is no fear she will embrace that lifestyle.

Amaryllis is at a low ebb right now, as Francesca declined her invitation, stating she's been inundated with patients in town.

Damien's mother was a physiotraducere, and since Francesca assumed the name of Whitmore, she's been determined to honour her adoptive grandmother by running the clinic she founded. I believe that's one of the major reasons Amaryllis and Damien waited this long to return to Haven. I have to admit, though, I'm overjoyed that they now live in the house over the river. Every time we meet, the bond between us as women, sisters, and mothers deepens.

I know Ammy keenly feels Francesca's absence, yet I also know that *she's Frannie's greatest champion. Her determination is why Damien and Ammy engaged the tutors for Francesca, ensuring her education was robust so she could undertake her medical training.*

Damien wishes she were closer so he could continue to guard her. He fears Travis Haven III could be out there, biding his time in the hopes of making us all pay for the loss of Haven House. My brother cannot ever be trusted.

The town is growing now. We've a second school and medical facilities to meet the needs of the families cast off by Haven House. Ammy and I have worked tirelessly with the women who were cast off before the dissolution of Haven House.

Those who were there on the fateful day I went to call have been given options. They can be trained to be useful in the community, to earn money so they can raise their children in the town they've called home. Not all have accepted that offer, but those who have are now living in houses provided for them by Andrew's company. There's still a divide in the community, but one day, I hope that too will be healed.

Ah, I hear Alexander on the stairs, and the steps of his nanny too, so I must close this before they enter the room and fill my life with happiness and childish chaos!

This morning I felt a stirring beneath my breast. This time I long for a daughter. A little girl for buttons and bows, perhaps? Perhaps we might be gifted with a woman who will rival Ammy and Francesca in drive, commitment, and honour.

I look forward to the coming adventure, as does my Andrew.

Gloriana Mulligan-Coultihan

Chapter One

I scanned the almost empty room. "Well, we've dealt with all the patients who presented this morning. Perhaps we should take some time, have a cup of tea and something to eat, before the afternoon sees the room fill again?"

Reginald sighed and swiped his hand over his forehead. "I don't know how you do it, Francesca. Every day, you run the clinic for those with cash to seek the enhancements, and then in the afternoon, you meet with those needing assistance for free. If it weren't for the Whitmore money, you wouldn't have the funds to keep this clinic open."

He regularly made this comment, and after the first few times, I'd explained that it was actually the money our morning patients brought in that paid for the work we did on the "charity cases," as he termed them. The Whitmore money was only invested in the clinic set-up, and belonged to my adoptive father, Damien Whitmore. I'd since given up trying to explain, as it was clear that it wasn't getting through to him.

Reginald might have been some four years my senior, but he'd only graduated from medical school last summer. As with many of the staff I now employed, he'd worked hard for his position. Unable to complete his studies full-time, he'd worked in the mortuary, preparing the deceased for their burials. It had paid well enough that he could afford the studies and kept food on the table for him and his three younger brothers. His mother worked as a washerwoman since his father died in an accident.

Jessie, my nurse assistant, bustled into the room. "Miss Francesca, the kettle is on the stove, and Millie is just back from the markets, about to make luncheon." She'd been a maid of Damien's before he and Ammy married and had wanted more.

"Thank you, Jessie." I hustled in behind her, hearing the *whirr-clank* of her replacement limb. "And before we see our first patient of the afternoon, I'll see you in my consulting room. I think you're due for a service."

Jessie opened her mouth, then closed it and nodded. "Yes, Miss Francesca."

Reginald flung himself into a chair. "You know, if you made people pay for servicing, we'd be a lot better off."

It was true, but I'd made it my mission to offer the poorest the best service available at prices they could afford. Every person on my afternoon client list had extended themselves to access the services we offered. "And you know our clients can't always afford it, Reggie. Besides, it's my choice to offer free servicing for the first five years."

He harrumphed and snatched up the paper, just as he always did when he lost an argument.

I lowered myself into the seat because on the front cover of the paper was a face I'd never forget. One that chilled me to the marrow.

Travis Haven III.

His face was ugly and distorted. My guts churned, but when Jessie returned and slid the tea in front of me, I was grateful. "Thank you," I whispered and wrapped my suddenly chilled fingers around the china cup, welcoming the sting of heat.

"Francesca?"

I started when Damien spoke from the door, and I rose and turned to glance at him, surprised he was here. "What are you doing here?"

His face was pale and grim. Though he was only in his early forties, his brow was creased with the lines of a man older. I had a fleeting second to wonder if some resulted from the injuries and issues my adoptive mother, Amaryllis, had overcome, worry for all of us children and the hard life he'd chosen before she had changed him. "I came as soon as Aloysius contacted me."

Aloysius was one of the many servants of the house, loyal to Damien, having stayed by his side during the attack on his home when I was little more than a teen. He remained in the home where Damien insisted I live, ensuring my privacy and safety.

"I didn't know until now." There was no reason I should pretend I didn't understand, but I could clearly see Reggie didn't know what we were talking about.

"Ammy also wanted me to check."

I moved to him, wrapped my arms around his middle, and placed my head against his chest. "Thank you," I murmured. "I'm fine, but knowing you're both so concerned"—I looked up, smiling into his concerned gaze—"makes me feel so much better."

Reginald stood and marched over, his brow now creased. "Mr Whitmore?"

Damien nodded, and Reginald's puffed-out chest seemed to deflate a little. "I came to check on Francesca here. With Travis Haven free, her safety is not assured."

Reginald opened his mouth, appearing like a floundering fish, before closing it tight and giving a harrumph as he cleared his throat.

Not for the first time, Reggie's reaction caused me to flinch, though I usually covered it. The shake of my hands betrayed my internal concerns. "Damien, I'm not sure..."

He shook his head. "You know Travis would get to Ammy if he could. Faith, Simeon, Constance, and Samson are safe. He can't get to them or Dawn. I can take care of myself, so that just leaves you."

I wished I could ignore the truth of his words, but I couldn't. "I have patients—"

He nodded slowly. "I understand. That's why I brought him."

A man stepped around the frame of the door. One I knew. I sucked my breath in.

"Miss Francesca." Raphael Nobel stood tall, his midnight-black hair shining in the sunlight and his face hewn as if from granite.

God, why now? my psyche almost screeched at me, because this was the one man I promised myself I'd never see again.

The last time I'd laid eyes on Raphael Nobel was at his father's funeral.

The grass crunched beneath my feet as I stepped toward the open grave. The cherry wood box which had been lowered held the remains of Adam Nobel. A man who'd spent countless hours with me, talking about the world and life.

He hadn't been a simple man. Neither had his life been blameless, yet I'd been drawn to him the way I guessed I would to a grandfather.

"Miss Francesca," a voice said behind me, cutting through the moment of introspection, and I turned.

Raphael Nobel was the second son of Adam. He wouldn't inherit the house that resembled a castle, nor the elaborate social structure of Nobel Crest. He'd already gone his own way, formed a group of inspectors working for the government.

"Mr Nobel." I waited for him to speak.

His grimace spoke volumes. "You'd become close with my father. He enjoyed your... company." In his eyes, something sparked. It could have been humour, but I had a suspicion it might be disgust too.

"I enjoyed talking with him. He sent me many books, and we corresponded frequently."

He inclined his head, and it was rather unnerving. "My father left a bequest for you."

I clutched my hands together. "What?"

Raphael's lips thinned. "Come now, you knew he'd leave you a gift, surely?"

I didn't really care for his attitude. Or the implication that I'd been encouraging a friendship in return for some reward. "Not at all. In fact, I'm surprised."

I didn't miss the way his gaze narrowed a little further. "Indeed. My brother has requested you meet with our man of business in the house when you're done here."

I cast a last look at the large hole. Adam's grave, I reminded myself, then turned away. "I shall go there directly."

I heard his footsteps echoing behind me and sighed. Some might call me cold; others whispered that I had some kind of illicit understanding with Adam. Only I knew the truth, and that was something I'd treasure and hold dear.

At the house, I entered while the staff watched me with cautious eyes. Unlike Haven House, there were women and men hired to ensure the upkeep of the building. Also unlike Haven House, the women were catered for in their own tiny homes. They weren't crowded in, nor were they cowed, but just because their conditions were kinder didn't make their situation any less dire in my mind.

They were still prisoners of a cult, even if the collars and cuffs were the softest ermine.

I entered the office, the large room smelling of must and cigars. The chair Adam had always filled sat behind the desk, and what I considered my chair was gone. By the fire waited Adam's heir, Edward. His clothes were an immaculate black, tailored to show off his trim physique.

He'd positioned himself with an elbow on the mantelpiece, his profile that of a polished man.

"So, Miss Francesca, come to collect your inheritance, I see." The bite in his words slid over me. I refused to allow him to denigrate me. I'd faced that so many times while growing up that it had hardened the shell I'd finally erected around my psyche.

"I was unaware Adam had made any provisions for me. There was no need."

Edward's lips thinned. "And yet he did." He moved to the desk, slid Adam's chair from the heavy wood table, and settled himself in it.

I noted the moment of discomfort and restrained my smile. Not as self-assured as he'd have me believe.

"So?" I demanded, more than a little aware that he was drawing this out, hoping to upset me.

"My father left the sum of three thousand dollars for your tuition. He claimed you planned to become a physiotraducere."

My refusal to acknowledge what he patently considered a spurious claim obviously irked him. His eyes flashed, and the knuckles of his hands whitened as he clenched his fists.

"He also left smaller sums for your siblings, Simeon, Sampson, Constance, and Faith. Could you perhaps enlighten me why?"

"Given I did not know he intended to leave funds for me, then I must answer, no, I do not."

He sneered. "He left this as well." Reaching into the drawer to the left-hand side, he withdrew a heavy envelope bulging at the sides. "I'm also to inform you that he's making a bequest to the Whitmore Foundation, on the proviso that should any members of Nobel Crest require care, you are to be the first called to duty in such matters."

That surprised me. I was unaware that any of the ladies of Nobel Crest had implantations, nor, from what Adam had led me to believe in the last months of his life, did the men. "I should like details of that bequest, of course. My father, the sheriff, will wish to check them with his legal counsel, I know."

He rose and grunted. "You have damaged the fabric of Nobel Crest. Before this, he would never have thought to release the wives from their duty, yet I am to ensure everyone knows they may leave, and further, that through the Whitmore Foundation, should they wish to learn skills and become emancipated, then I am to ensure they have those opportunities." His voice turned waspish; his face screwed up. "I don't know what power you held over our father, but you have done evil every day since he laid eyes on you, so take your ill-gotten proceeds and leave this place. Never return. Should our people need your assistance, we will transport them to you." He fairly quivered with outrage, and it buffeted me.

I inclined my head, because I'd told nothing but the truth.

Turning on the ball of my foot, I faltered slightly. Raphael's gaze bored down on me, and I felt jabs of hate from Edward as well. I would not give them the satisfaction of seeing me fall; instead, I pasted a smile on my face and walked from the room.

Raphael followed, I knew. No doubt making sure I don't steal the silver or corrupt the women, *I thought with harsh insight. I heard his footsteps behind me as I headed for the front door.*

"Your things have already been loaded onto the dirigible," he offered.

"Then I shall leave." I allowed myself to turn back, just once, sweeping my gaze over the building, committing it to memory. Then I turned in the cemetery's direction. Knots of people gathered at the gates, no doubt reminiscing about Adam Nobel.

Without another word, I stepped aboard.

"Miss Francesca." The captain hurried forth. "It's good to have you aboard. Would you care to retire to the lounge?"

"No, I'll stay here."

And that's exactly what I did as the craft rose slowly into the air. I watched as Nobel Crest and Raphael Nobel became specks before I retreated.

I shook my head, trying to clear away the veil that had settled over my mind. Raphael Nobel was here, in front of me. "Father? I don't need... I've got Aloysius—"

"Who is old. Slow. He keeps the house security in line, and under normal circumstances, I'd have no qualms. But this is Travis Haven. A very dangerous and devious man, Frannie." His face crinkled with concern. He might have only been in his early forties, but the hard life he'd chosen as a sheriff and lawman had taken its toll. Wrinkles at his brow and eyes betrayed the depth of his concern.

Reginald harrumphed, and we turned en masse. "Do you really think he would attempt something like that here? I know you have a checkered past, Francesca, but it's not like—"

"Her mother, Amaryllis, almost died because of his actions. We know of at least four deaths we can directly attribute to him." My father's blunt words had Reginald paling. The little man at the table dragged a handkerchief from his pocket and mopped his brow now that he was aware of the danger.

"Father," I implored, hoping he'd understand my concern. "I'm not in danger, but if I were and accepted security, there's no need for—"

"Me?" I heard the tension in Raphael's voice and contained a wince.

"We need to talk, Frannie," Damien continued. "Your office might be best."

That sense of unreality enfolded me as I stumbled to my consulting room, holding the door until my father and Raphael entered. Then I pushed the door closed gently, tottered to my desk, and settled in the wooden chair.

"There's more. We've received threats, Francesca—" Damien began.

"Credible threats," Raphael growled, cutting in. "He's been watching you or having someone do so. We have times and places of your locations day to day combined with the letters. Your father checked your whereabouts at those times with Aloysius."

I blinked once, then again. "I... Well, that's not normal, is it?"

Damien shook his head. "No. My concern is he can't get to us, so you're the one he's fixated on."

"And you're sure?"

"Yes. I would stay with you, Francesca, but Ammy's increasing again."

"Ah." I nodded, knowing Damien's concerns for his wife and pregnancy. "And she needs you." My guts churned. Damien couldn't give me security himself, so the option he was suggesting meant I'd have to accept Raphael for the term of the investigation and neutralisation of the threat.

Damien nodded.

"Then I will grudgingly accept Mr Nobel's presence for the moment." I didn't want to and thus couldn't help if the words sounded terse. I closed my eyes, inhaled deeply. Then, once more balanced, I opened them and glanced at Raphael Nobel. His face was as it had been, finely hewn, with a sharp jaw, a flash of jet-black hair, and grey-green eyes I was sure could see his very soul in. His lips, full as they may be, were tight with disapproval. "Mr Nobel, welcome to the Whitmore Foundation." I reached out my hand, hoping to at least calm the storm which seemed to always be there when we were both in attendance.

"Miss Whitmore." He nodded.

"*Dr* Whitmore," I corrected and saw the flare of recognition in his eyes. I wasn't sure what he thought I'd done in the intervening years, but based on his expression, it certainly hadn't been achieving a medical degree.

"My apologies, Doctor."

Damien cleared his throat, and I looked back at him. "You probably need to get back, but let Jessie at least prepare refreshments," I said.

He smiled. "Always time for you, Francesca. I'm sorry—"

I read the sorrow in his eyes and smiled. "I know. She's fragile. I understand, Father." I didn't use the title often enough, but when I did, it was always honest, and I was rewarded with a smile and hug.

* * *

Once Damien left, and I was assured he'd at least eaten something, I relaxed enough to watch Raphael interrogate Reggie. There wasn't a more appropriate term, I thought.

"You travel by coach here every morning. Your *own* coach?"

Reggie squirmed, and I took pity on him, answering in his stead. "His grandmother is Elizabeth Squires, daughter of Emmett Squires of Squires Mills." His eyes widened. "Reggie is the third son, and while he could have lived a life of leisure, he wanted to work in medicine." I couldn't help but notice the flash of red on his cheeks. He was a proud man, but he was disconnected from the day-to-day grind of the lower classes, as he constantly called them.

"Ah," Raphael answered. "So yes, I can see why you came in a private carriage. Tell me, has anyone ever approached you regarding Miss..." He sighed. "Doctor Whitemore's whereabouts?"

Reggie sneered. "Only the eligible men who've requested her company at soirees."

It was hard to bite back a laugh at his answer, so instead I stood, swiping an invisible dot of lint from my tunic. "I believe it's time to prepare for the afternoon list. Reggie, would you be a dear and send Jessie to my office with the charts?"

I knew Raphael followed me to my office without even glancing behind me. "Mr Nobel, Reggie is a trustworthy person. I personally selected him to work with me at the foundation," I explained, settling into my chair.

"Your safety is the reason I was sent here by Damien. Anyone with contact could be the person who's feeding Travis Haven details of your timetable." His words dripped with derision, and I clenched my hands into tight fists before releasing the pressure.

Instead of an outburst, I nodded, aware that Damien wouldn't request this of me without a cause. In all the years I'd known him, he wasn't one to cry danger without having some shred of evidence. Still, I didn't enjoy having Raphael, who'd watched his brother call my actions into question, in my life and in such proximity. "While I see the why, you must understand—"

"Look, you don't want me here. I'm not overly enthused with this task, but Damien specifically requested me. He said you were aware of the task force, so I can speak freely. Haven is dangerous and fixated. He will end you if he can get near enough. We need to overcome the friction that exists between us, Miss Francesca. He wants a way to get back at Amaryllis and Damien for destroying Haven House and the township he and his father built as an edifice to their cult."

The way he said my name incensed me. "I'm no child, Mr Nobel. I have a life, a calling, and while I appreciate your task, I will not allow it to rule my life. Now, what I require from you are the details of your engagement."

"Dammit, listen to me. You are the target but not the reason for the danger. Your parents—"

"I know exactly what they did, Mr Nobel. I was there. An innocent caught up in the Haven House mess. I know exactly what those cults do, the damage they wreak on the innocent, and the way they don't care about the children." I wanted to say more but didn't. I'd learned restraint, and though it cost me dearly, I didn't add that Nobel Crest was no better.

As if he could read my thoughts, a red tide crested his cheeks. "I—"

I raised a hand as a knock came at my door. "Enter," I called, aware he was infuriated that I'd cut him off.

Jessie entered the room, her arms full of patient folios. "Miss Francesca, the patients have arrived. I've gone through the list, and their folders are in order of their appointments."

"Thank you, Jessie. Could you perhaps escort Mr Nobel back to the dining room, where he can wait—"

"No," he growled.

"Well, you can't stay in here. My patients expect and are entitled to their privacy," I returned.

"Not in the dining room. Find me somewhere in the waiting room, at the very least."

"You'll terrify my patients unless you have something to do." I couldn't help but scan him. The suit he wore was well fitting, but it didn't hide his heavy gun belt or the bulge of his shoulders. He was an imposing man.

"I have a book in my bag. I can read," he uttered through clenched teeth.

I sighed heavily. "Jessie, could you ask Miles and Thorne to carry in an armchair from the private consulting room? Mr Nobel will wait in the patient hall. Ensure he has tea or coffee at regular intervals."

Jessie nodded, though I didn't miss the speculation keen in her gaze. "Yes, Doctor."

She scurried away, and I rose. "My appointments begin in ten minutes. I need time to prepare. If you'd please step out of the room?"

I turned toward the pile Jessie had delivered, took up the first folder, and sighed once more. I knew this patient well.

Chapter Two

I rubbed the back of my neck, letting the exhaustion of a day well employed wash over me. As I closed the last folder, a shout came from beyond the door. Rushing forward, I grasped the knob, wrenched open the door, and stepped into the hall.

A girl, crying out in pain as blood dripped from beneath her gown, was being carried in. Raphael watched, his face white.

"Bring her in here," I urged and hurried them into my office. All too often, this would happen. An injured child was brought to me as the parents knew I'd see them without cost.

I grabbed one of the large aprons I usually wore in such situations and donned it, then hurried to the sink, washed my hands, and inhaled deeply.

"Let me see," I whispered as the man laid the girl on the pallet.

I lifted her gown to reveal a bloodied mass of flesh and bone.

"What happened?" I enquired as I set about inspecting deeper while the girl writhed in pain. The injury was bad.

"We were crossing at the railroad when a vehicle hit her. My Holly, she flew onto the tracks. There was wire embedded, and it..." He gulped.

I continued to palpate the area of the injury. "I can save her leg, but it will require surgery. I take it you don't have funds?"

He tugged the cap from his head and gripped it in both hands, his face pale and sweaty. *Oh, please don't pass out.* "Miss, I... She's my only child."

I nodded. "Go out in the hall. My assistants, Jessie and Miles, are required. Tell them I need tincture of morphine and chloroform. Hurry now," I urged him out, then turned back to the child. "It's okay. I'm going to help you, but you must lie still for now."

She mewled, and I could understand her fear. If she was ten, I'd be surprised. Such pain regularly overcame adults, let alone children who didn't know what I was about to do. "It hurts," she sobbed.

"I know. I'm going to make you have a sleep, and then I'm going to fix it," I soothed, hoping Jessie and Miles were quick.

The door opened, and they bustled in, hands filled with cases of instruments and the items I'd requested. Miles settled in to prepare the chloroform, and Jessie was setting up to prepare for the task ahead. While I had an excellent office set-up, emergencies always required items we kept locked in a pharmacological room to ensure their safety.

Once the child slept, I reached out. "We need to move the bed into a better position." Thankfully it was on wheels, so we trundled it around, ensuring it was in the centre of the room, allowing me full access to the limb, and I got to work, cleaning the area, then setting the broken bone into position. The flesh was torn and would take hours to suture, so I set about the task, working layer by layer, heartened that none of the major veins had sustained damage.

When the task was completed, we wrapped the injury with bandages before I allowed myself to sink into the chair with a sigh. My back ached as it often did from such wearying endeavours, and I massaged it while I waited for the child's parent to enter the room.

"Is she...?" He gulped and looked at the restful figure on the bed.

"She sleeps. We sedated her. It was a nasty break, but I've set it. She needs to be kept as still as possible, and I'll need to visit in the next few days to check the healing. You must keep an eye out for infection, temperature, and so on. If you have any concerns, bring her back here or send word for the Whitmore Foundation."

His face creased and shoulders slumped. "I... Her mother died just ten months ago. She's all I have left, and—"

I rose and slid my arms around his shoulders. "She'll make a full recovery. But she needs quiet, good food, and care. Can you offer her those?"

He shook his head. "The room we have is in a boarding house. I've been looking for work and…"

His worry was palpable, a veritable stink in the air. "We can assist with that. Jessie, my nurse and assistant, can find accommodation with one of the charitable associations hereabouts. Several have agreements with us. They will house you both and offer sustenance. They may also assist you in finding work. Go see her just outside, as you can't leave until the child wakes."

He left me then, and I sighed. I had once been in a similar situation. Memories of the tiny hovel where we'd lived with Mama were always there, in the back of my mind. We'd been brought low when she'd become ill, and it was the charitable associations there which had brought Amaryllis and Damien into my life. I was a walking and talking advertisement that sometimes charity worked.

The door opened, and Raphael stepped into the room. "Are you…?"

"What are you doing in here?" I demanded, rising from my seat.

"Checking on you. It's been hours, and you've yet to have a break." His face was shadowed, and I glanced at the clock on the wall. Eleven o'clock.

"I have to wait for her to wake, then check her. Plus, we need to wait for assistance to find them somewhere safe and clean to stay." I rubbed my eyes, aware of my sudden drop in energy.

"Couldn't someone else—"

I shook my head. "No. I'm the head of the facility. This is my task, and as it is, I still can't send Jessie or Miles home just yet, either."

"Then you should at least have something to eat. Take a break, and get someone to sit with her and call you when she wakes."

A sound from the bed had me rising from the chair. "She's waking now. Ask her father to come in, and then give us some privacy, please."

* * *

The child woke slowly, her father hovering by the side of the bed. I waited, sitting quietly in the chair. The girl was young but old enough to have me explain the situation.

Her cry when she was aware enough told me it was time to make my presence known. "Hello. I'm the doctor who attended to your leg. Do you remember me?"

The girl, Holly, looked at me with large dark eyes. "Did I...? Is my leg going to be okay?"

I knew what she was asking and squeezed her hand. "It's a terrible break, but it will get better in time. Your father and I plan to move you to a recuperation house." She started to rise, so I pressed firmly on her chest. "Holly, you won't be alone. Your father will go with you and stay there. I'll visit in a day or so to check your injury."

Tears spilled down her pale cheeks. "But he has to find work."

I nodded, keeping my face neutral. "Yes. But while you're there, they will assist him to find a job and help you both find a home so you can build a safe future."

She probably didn't understand, and I remembered back to when I was her age. My mother was ill, her second "husband" was dead, and she had multiple mouths to feed. Times were tough and money scarce. I understood her fears all too well.

Turning to Holly's father, I implored him to make her understand that all would be well so long as they did as was asked.

"It'll be okay, Holly love. They're going to help us, and you're going to be well again. Just wait and see. One day, we'll have us a tiny house, and you can be a lady, just like your mama wanted." He hunched over the girl on the bed, swiping an unsteady hand at Holly's face.

A rap came at the door, and I opened it. Jessie handed me a note. "They'll be waiting outside. Miles and her father can carry the pallet and lay her on the seat."

I unsuccessfully tried to fend off a yawn and relayed the information before stepping back so Miles and Jessie could prepare Holly for transporting, ensuring she was adequately covered with a blanket. Then Miles gave instructions to her father, and Jessie followed them out.

When the room was empty, I made the last notes in the file, inordinately aware that Raphael had returned and watched me.

I took my time closing the file, then straightening my desk. Finally I rose and turned, removing my soiled apron and coat and setting them on the bed.

Jessie appeared, my coat in her hand.

"Jessie, in the morning, you send Lily in. Do not come in until at least ten." The girl nodded her acceptance of my order. "And tell Miles he's not to come in until then, either. Send for Carl. He can fill in tomorrow. He wanted more experience, he said."

Raphael took the coat from Jessie, and I shrugged into it, not wanting him near me. But what other option was there? I'd agreed with Damien that I would allow him to act as my bodyguard, and I kept my promises, no matter how hard they were to keep.

"You're ready now?" His voice played over my exhausted brain like a sudden violin in silence.

"Yes." I moved toward the door.

"What about Reginald?"

I turned, his question surprising me. "He would have gone home hours ago. I don't ask him to stay back and assist in emergency cases like this."

Raphael opened the door, revealing the carriage ready and waiting, as I knew Jessie would have arranged. I waited as he opened the door to our conveyance before climbing inside. Exhaustion settled over me like a heavy weight, but I wouldn't give in just yet. When I was home and safely within my bedchamber, then I'd let it wash me away.

"Why?" He'd followed me into the dark confines.

I wrinkled my brow. "He's not aligned to the foundation apart from as an employee. His grandmother would love him to form a relationship with me, and initially, it's why he came to work here. But I never wished to encourage that, so I never requested his help. It didn't seem right when I had no..." I struggled to find a word.

"Designs on him?" Raphael queried.

I nodded and covered another yawn with a hand. "Yes."

"So instead you fill the gaps alone, running yourself ragged."

"I didn't know you cared," I quipped tiredly, letting my eyes close. Conserving my energy, I tried to tell myself, but the truth was they were heavy, and I just needed to last the next ten minutes or so before I could collapse.

That small act cost me, because when I opened them, I was in Raphael's arms, standing at the door to my home.

"Put me down," I asked.

"You're exhausted. Tell me which room, and then you can sleep." There was a tension about him I hadn't noticed before, along with the breadth of his chest and the strength of his arms.

"Please, Mr Nobel," I started, but I could hear the weariness myself there in my words.

"Raphael," he corrected. "Which room?"

The door opened. Aloysius stared at the sight of me held in a man's arms. "Miss Francesca?" His face was heavily lined and his limp more pronounced, likely because of tiredness.

"I'm fine. I fell asleep in the carriage, it seems." I smiled, though my eyes felt gritty. "Mr Nobel, you can put me down now."

He did, and I swayed. His arm wound around my waist to steady me. I would have pulled away, but I'd likely fall. "Stubborn woman."

"Doctor," I reminded him with some asperity, and this time, he laughed.

"As you wish, *Dr* Whitmore."

I removed my coat and handed it to Aloysius. "I'll wish to leave by eight, so call breakfast for seven, if you could."

He bowed. "Of course, Miss Francesca. I've also made up a chamber for Mr Nobel next to you. The blue room was the one Mr Whitmore suggested. Your bags were delivered this afternoon, sir. I've also had light refreshments prepared, and they'll be sent up to your room. Miss Francesca, when we received news from Jessie, we had the bath prepared for you."

"Oh, bless you, Aloysius. Yes, a bath will be perfect."

When I reached the steps, I laid a hand on the wooden balustrade, the same one I'd held years ago as we ran down the steps in our headlong flight. I closed my eyes, hoping it wouldn't be like that again.

I made my way up the stairs, aware of Raphael following me the whole way, and turned to the left, heading for the family wing, as Damien had laughingly called it years ago. My room was the third door.

Damien and Amaryllis had insisted I should have a larger suite, and while the first two rooms were spacious, they weren't as lushly appointed as the one I used.

Raphael's would be the second one, the blue room. I opened the door. "This is your room. I'm sure everything you need is here. However, there is a button just here to call for assistance." I pointed to the large black button above the switch for the lights.

"And you're next door?" He pointed to the one by the stairs.

"No. The other side." I pointed to my door and made to retreat, but before I could back away, he grabbed my hand.

"Sleep well, Francesca. Tomorrow, we should talk."

I watched his face, saw something move in his eyes. An emotion deep and somehow compelling. Something that pierced me with fear. "Perhaps over breakfast."

Then I did retreat, and while I didn't hear his door shut, I rather guessed he'd waited till I was safely within my room before he closed it.

Chapter Three

Morning came far too soon, but today being a normal workday, there was no chance to rest and relax.

I swung my feet from the bed and rose, stretched the muscles in my back, arms, and legs, then retreated to my bathing room. This was indeed a luxury, but my father was insistent that with the long hours and community services I provided, I should be able to have such privacy.

After washing my face, I settled to tame my bird's nest hair. It curled naturally, and it seemed to take longer each day to unknot it. More than once, I'd considered hacking it off. "It would be easier after long nights," I muttered, attacking a persistent knot. Amaryllis would be unhappy but accepting if I did so, and the notion teased at the corners of my mind again.

Finally satisfied with the hair arrangement I achieved, I dressed in one of my workday gowns. A simple grey-and-silver buttoned affair of wool, not too close-fitting, and thankfully this one had a light corset built in, so it was more realistic for my role. My boots were comfortable, leather with an insert of wool to cushion my feet.

With a last look in the mirror, I rose, ready to face the day and mostly ready for Raphael Nobel and whatever he'd wanted to say last night.

But when I settled at the table, no one was present. In silence, I poured coffee and ate my fill of toast, then rose.

Aloysius stepped forward. "Mr Nobel informed me that he has received some grievous news and was required to travel home. He insists you remain home today." On his face was a kind of resignation. He knew what I was about to say, and while he didn't like it, he understood my reasoning. Or so I guessed.

"I'm sorry, Aloysius. You know I can't. However, perhaps you will travel with me?" I rarely made such requests, not wanting to upset the running of the household, but I'd promised my father that I'd take the danger seriously. "I have a light patient load today. Only three private patients, then a few of the foundation appointments. I intend to be home by lunchtime."

"Of course, Miss Francesca. I will inform Mrs Langtree and will have David fill my role during our absence."

The older man hurried away, and for the first time, I considered just how much pressure I was likely putting on him. He had to be in his fifth decade, with silver sprinkled through his immaculately combed-back hair. He was still large and imposing, the main reason I'd always counted on him as a bodyguard should I need one, but now I realised others may see him as weak.

I made a mental note to raise this with my adoptive parents.

Once more readied for the clinic, I climbed into the carriage. Aloysius refused my offer to sit within and took up a seat with the coachman. A few moments later, I felt the lurch as the horseless carriage rolled forward.

* * *

The following day, I rested in the library's chair, book in hand, while a cup of tea cooled beside me. Sundays were the one day I allowed myself to rest, and I luxuriated in waking late and eating food that wasn't always the most nutritious but tasty.

A knock came at the door, and I called for the person to enter.

"This just arrived, Miss Francesca, via the wireless telegraph," Aloysius explained.

I opened the folded page and smiled.

Dearest sister,
Mama and Papa have said that I'm to be granted a year in
London once I conclude my studies to improve my knowledge of
clothing manufacturing. I'm overjoyed by this news. They've
added the caveat that I must wait until the Travis Haven situa-
tion is completed.
I have no recollection of him, yet Mama says he's a nasty man.
Dangerous and untrustworthy. We don't leave the grounds
without what Papa deems an acceptable escort. Faith and I visited
town just yesterday, and we had to have five armed guards. It
seems overzealous.
Faith reminded me to have you find a copy of Errant Silversmiths:
Artists who Bend the Boundaries *for her. She claims this is the*
most groundbreaking tome for smiths, and she simply cannot live
without it. Mama reminds me to say "Come home soon." She
wishes she could travel, but with her "interesting condition," Papa
is adamant the home is the best place for her.
The baby is now walking, and our brothers continue to be as
annoying as usual. Simeon taps at the harpsichord for many
hours. He's gained quite the repertoire, and the ladies of the town
are most engaged in listening to him almost daily. Though, to be
fair, he's also wishful of learning the craft of engineering, so he
may be useful to our father.
Sampson now spends long hours with our uncle, learning the trade
of artificer, and we rarely see him daily. I know Uncle Andrew
will encourage him to take control of the Coultihan Manufactory
before long.
Your correspondence also lacks. Papa indicated you were well but
busy when he was there this week, but I long to hear tales of the
city, the soirées you attend (infrequently), and the latest on dit. Do
reply soon.
Your loving, though slightly cross, sister,
Constance

"Oh, Constance. I wish I had news for you," I muttered, folding the paper and sliding it into the pocket of my gown.

As I did so, another knock caught my attention, and I raised my head.

Raphael Nobel strode into the room, his face tight.

"Mr Nobel. So you have returned."

"Indeed, Miss... Dr Whitmore." He took the seat opposite me. "You don't run the clinic today?"

I inclined my head. "Even the staff and I must take time to rest and recharge our bodies."

"Indeed." He held himself still as he sat opposite me, and I wondered if I had somehow insulted him.

"Mr Nobel, something appears to be amiss." I wouldn't ask what, because that would be prying, and with him, that was the last thing I wished to be accused of, on top of the long-standing accusation of being a gold digger.

Oh, how the memory of that day burned me still!

"Yes. My brother has taken ill."

I stayed quiet. He had many brothers, two full-blooded and innumerable halves scattered around the small town where Nobel Crest was situated.

"You are unlike other women, Miss Francesca."

His words startled me. "Why?"

"Most would ask which. You do not. Is it you don't care or that you wish to appear unconcerned or...?" He let the words hang in the air.

"Should you wish me to know which, you will tell me when you're ready, Mr Nobel."

He snorted. "Raphael, as we both agreed you'd use." Then he sighed heavily and slumped into the seat. "My younger brother Ellis is ill. He had an accident some months ago, but the injury didn't heal."

"What does the physician say?"

"Edward wouldn't allow a physician to be called, or at least not one with the skills required."

Sudden dread filled me. "A physiotraducere?"

Raphael nodded. "I wasn't there and haven't returned to Nobel Crest for many months. My work takes me elsewhere for extended periods of time. Miss Francesca, Ellis is but eighteen, too young to pass from the injuries, but he needs assistance. Will you…?" He swallowed deeply, and I noted the tremor of his hands as he gripped the arms of the chair.

I bit my lip, glancing at the clock. "I will need Jessie to prepare my bag, and she may need to accompany me, along with Miles. I can send word to my patients." I stood and brushed down the cream dress I wore, brain whirring with rapidly evolving lists. "I need an hour or two, and then we can be on our way."

I'd promised Adam, all those years ago, that I would stand by Nobel Crest. I would keep my word, even if Edward was there.

As I marched to the door, I heard Raphael rise and step toward me.

"Miss Francesca?"

I pivoted in the doorway, glancing back at his face.

"My brother Edward, he regrets his words from that day," he offered.

I nodded, because there really wasn't much else I could say that would fix the situation the two brothers had wrought with such care-lessness, then moved swiftly into the hallway.

Chapter Four

I t never ceased to amaze me the speed at which the dirigibles covered distances. The steady *whir, whir, whir* filled the air as I glanced out the large window at the lush land below. Tiny specks of houses and people passed beneath us as we travelled under fluffy white clouds.

"Tea, Miss Francesca?" I only vaguely remembered Jarvis from the long-ago visits to and from Adam Nobel's.

I also knew that during that time, many questions were asked why a young girl my age, with no appreciable connection to him, would visit him and vice versa. Jarvis had always been there, silently following the man. He'd been in attendance many times when Adam had insisted. I should never have felt the need to explain, yet I'd known the whispers took place because of the way their voices would hush when I entered a room.

Jarvis had never looked at me with those questions in his eyes, though, and his presence made the journey back to Nobel Crest—the first to the house in the long years since Adam's passing—a little easier. I'd not stepped foot within the gates since Adam died because of Edward's decree, though I had tried once. It was enough to remind me that I was only there on sufferance.

"Thank you, Jarvis. It's good to see you again," I added.

He grinned, face creasing. "You too, miss. You haven't been near Nobel Crest for nearly a year and not within the house proper for years. There are many who have sorely missed you."

"And those who would wish me to the very devil."

Now he sobered. "Those who spoke badly of you never took the time to know your story, miss. They're either bitter and twisted or those who grieved."

I accepted the cup he placed in my hand, considering his words. If it had only been months since Adam's death, I might agree with the second half, but as it was, Edward had never trusted me. Neither had the wives and daughters. That had become even more pronounced after his death.

Adam had asked for my help in those last months, as he knew the end was close. He'd wanted me to work with the wives who wished to break away from the clan, and I'd agreed. Even then, I'd taken up the mantle of working with the Whitmore Foundation, and today, many of those assisting the less fortunate were those who'd left Nobel Crest.

One in particular, Almira, who was closer to my age, unofficially handled the housing of the less fortunate, particularly women fleeing from dangerous situations, such as many had faced during Haven House's rise and eventual fall.

"We'll be landing soon, Miss Francesca. If you'd care to use the retiring room, I can escort you."

"Thank you, Jarvis." I rose, tugging my reticule close and following him to the lush bathroom outfitted with a deep chaise, sink, and even a bath, the room shining and spotless.

From my bag, I tugged a small brush, then unpinned my hair and brushed it out before twisting and repinning it in place.

My gown was unblemished, a creamy moire decorated with dark blue embroidery. My coat, a three-quarter-length wool, kept me warm at this altitude but would likely be too much once we'd landed. I remembered well the humid days of summer at Nobel Crest and the way the nights only took a touch of chill.

Now, prepared for whatever Edward Nobel might say, I returned to the waiting room, startling when I noted Raphael had joined me.

"I didn't think I'd see you before we landed," I murmured, and he glanced sharply at me.

"I was replying to some business, though I'm sure I explained I'd return as soon as I could."

Not that he had, but I felt a little more comforted to know he'd be by my side on our arrival. Jessie and Miles had both decided they'd stay in the dining room, and I understood their need for privacy. They'd been wed not quite a year, and it seemed to me that though they always comported themselves with propriety, allowing them quiet time alone meant that when I truly needed them, they understood the urgency of any task set.

I'd agreed they should join me upon landing so we would enter the grounds of Nobel Crest together. I trusted Jessie's instincts, and Miles, big and burly as he was, would protect Jessie and me. If I had to choose my family, they'd be among it.

The sound of the engines altered, and I felt the moment we changed course and dipped lower in the sky. I dropped into the seat, tugging on the ribbons to fasten myself in, not that I expected more than a tiny jolt as we contacted the earth.

Long moments passed, and then we landed. I followed Raphael to the gangplank and smiled at Jessie and Miles when they joined us, their eyes shining. "Miss Francesca, Miles has arranged for our bags to be delivered to the hotel."

Raphael frowned. "Hotel? You're coming with me to Nobel Crest."

I cleared my throat. "I'm forbidden to visit Nobel Crest. Your brother didn't just say that, he ensured I would be denied access. The only time I attempted to enter, I was barred from the gates. The hotel will suit my needs, anyway. I imagine your brother is at the infirmary?"

His face shuttered, and I wondered what was going on behind his grey-green eyes. Did he not realise that as the master of Nobel Crest, when his brother made that pronouncement, it became law?

"My brother lives in his own home, on the grounds. Surely you can—"

Miles stepped forward. "I was with Dr Whitmore that day. I can assure you, when she says the gates were barred, she does not overstate the reality."

"Come. If he's not in the infirmary, then he must be moved there. Then I will have the resources to attend to his needs," I said, deciding the best option right now was to break through the freezing impasse of his brother's edict. "It's quite new and well resourced. If he can be brought to me today, I can devise a treatment plan."

His nod was tight, and I couldn't miss the waves of fury ripping through the air.

Together, once the way was cleared, we strode down the planks and into the small township. It wasn't quite the bustling place I remembered, and I couldn't help but frown, glancing at the empty shop windows. "Where is everyone?"

"I don't...," Raphael murmured. "It's like they've all just left."

The hotel, standing at the end of the row, was dark, the doors shut. Wind whistled down a tunnel of street, sheets of paper tumbling about end on end as a chill caught the air.

Raphael rapped his knuckles on the door once and waited, then a second time.

The door squeaked open after the rattling sound of a key turning. "Master Raphael, come in. Your friends... Miss... Dr Francesca, you're a sight for sore eyes." Oscar, the portly hotel manager, bowed and ushered us within.

"What is happening, Oscar?"

The man winced at Raphael's curt demand.

"Master Edward gave the order. We were to either return to Nobel Crest or vacate the shops, sir."

Raphael's face blanked. "When was this order given?"

"Just this morning. We had hours to either close and return to the Crest or go."

"This morning?" Raphael asked as if it was a personal blow.

"Yes, sir. The doctor, sir, he has no like of her. Master Edward hasn't, either. When he heard she was coming, I heard he flew into a rage. Demanded we all ensure no one was here to make her welcome. He's also given orders that your brother is not to attend the infirmary, sir. But he doesn't want you to hear it from one of us."

Raphael tensed. "I'll sort this out. Find rooms for us, whatever is needed, and organise meals. I'm going to travel to Nobel Crest myself. Find me a horse."

The man winced. "Begging your pardon, but he requisitioned them all this morning. There aren't any left here."

"Fine, I'll walk," he growled.

* * *

I sat on my bed, wondering what would happen next. Edward's intransigence cost lives, I knew that, but concern for Raphael's and Edward's younger brother left my skin crawling. He hadn't chosen to live this life, and from memory, he'd been a slight and scholarly boy.

When Edward had assumed the mantle of leading the clan, he'd bought into the status and power, and it had fed his ego.

Raphael, well, he was different. So different, and I didn't quite know how to deal with it. I wanted to hold on to my fury with him, given what had passed, but with every action, that was becoming harder.

That Damien trusted him confused me. My father trusted few, and those he did had earned it a dozen times over. I racked my brain trying to work out if my father had named him, spoke of his deeds, but I came up with nothing.

"Dammit, Frannie, this makes no sense," I chided myself, rising and pacing the length of the room.

Underlying my confusion was an interest I desperately wished to avoid. I didn't need a man. I was a strong and well-educated woman. "And that sounds pretty damn hollow right now," I muttered. I didn't hide in my room, vacillating; this just wasn't me. Yet what exactly did I want? "Don't even consider it," I growled as my door opened.

I whirled, skirts swirling around my ankles, and stared as Raphael entered the room, his face more tightly drawn than before.

"What? Where is Ellis?"

"He's being transported to the infirmary. Francesca, he won't let you into Nobel Crest. But there are women who need your help." It sounded like he'd bitten some sour fruit. His expression twisted.

"What do you mean? Raphael?"

"He had them punished, Francesca. Whipped."

My guts froze. "Wha... No. Surely not. Your father was always adamant—"

"And Edward is no Adam Nobel, Francesca." He shrugged, and I could clearly see the vulnerability and pain.

"Come, then, let's see to your brother first. Then we'll make a plan." And indeed, I knew just how to achieve it.

I grabbed my cardigan and slid my arms into it, thankful I'd removed my heavier coat, then snatched up my medical bag from where Miles had deposited it.

We moved at a quick pace and had just arrived at the small building at the end of the road when a dray pulled up alongside. In the middle, on a pallet, was a pale, fine young man, his face ravaged by pain, sweat beading his lips. "Francesca... you... came."

If it hadn't been for my training, I'd have wept. "I will always come, Ellis. We need him inside. Lift the pallet carefully." I dragged the heavy key from my skirt pocket and opened the building, pleased it was at least clean. "Bring him through to the consulting room, and I'll take over from there."

/

Chapter Five

Rage filled me. I couldn't categorically state that at this point Ellis would survive. His body was racked with infection, and while I'd administered what I could, it would be touch-and-go.

I'd lanced the wound site and drained the built-up fluid, which stank. I'd cleansed his body as best I could, difficult even with Miles's help. Now, settled in a clean gown, he rested in the bed while I watched over him.

Raphael sat in a chair on the opposite side of his bed, his gaze never leaving his brother's face.

"He's going to be here for a while," I told him. "You should go rest."

The droop of his mouth reminded me that I'd never seen him so cast down. "I'll stay, if it's all the same."

I rose. "All right, then. Miles is just outside the door if you need him. If there's any change or his fever spikes, send for me. I'm going into the other room to see the women."

The glint in his eyes turned cold. "I will make him pay for this."

I sighed. "Perhaps so, but right now, your brother and those women are my priority. If you need to leave, send Miles in to sit with him."

Bustling from the room took every ounce of my willpower because some part of my inner core insisted he needed me right now. But so did the women. I was torn.

Jessie had the women, who'd slunk in over the last hour, sequestered in a small room across the hall. I entered, then stilled as the wailing and physical evidence of their pain hit me.

One girl I knew half rose, then slumped back down. "Miss Francesca. Thank heavens you're here."

Advancing quickly, I reached her side and helped her to stand before urging her to the bed behind a screen. "Do you want me to conduct the exam with the other women in here?"

She nodded with frantic moves. "Yes. We're safer together."

Biting my lip so I wouldn't make a comment I'd regret, I simply helped her to the bed and set about unfastening her gown.

Thankfully she didn't wear a corset, but it was obvious she'd received less nourishment lately. "Have you been eating well?" I enquired.

She stiffened. "When we break one of the master's rules, he refuses us food. I seem to speak out of turn a lot," she whispered.

Below the fabric, I could clearly see long welts and bruises. "A cane?" I asked.

"Yes," she whispered.

"Anything else?"

The way she stilled and her breathing shallowed had me closing my eyes. "Rape?"

"He doesn't call it that. It's 'punishment by submission,' as he says." Her voice was thready, filled with congealed sorrow.

Burning rage rose in my breast. "It's rape. No man has the right to force himself upon you. Your cycle?"

"Late."

I helped her to dress and settled her into a chair, made a note on her chart, then moved on to the next woman.

During the day, ten women arrived at the door, all telling the same story. Aged between eighteen and twenty, I knew at least two were pregnant and suspected with the first girl I'd seen.

Jessie ushered them to the hotel and would head to town with us when we left. The dirigible we'd travelled in belonged to Raphael personally, so at least Edward wouldn't be able to countermand that action when we left.

The whole time I remained at the infirmary, I knew the moment was drawing ever closer to disclose the final request Adam had made of me. It gnawed at my mind, because I knew the damage it would inflict.

By the end of the day, Ellis had grown worse, and I returned to the ward where he rested. He thrashed on the bed while Raphael remained at his side, talking to him soothingly, bathing his forehead.

"The women?"

I shook my head. "I'll explain later. For now, they're safe at the hotel. You should take some time and eat. Take a rest. I'll need you here later."

Not that I wanted him gone, but I feared we'd need to evacuate before Edward got wind. I wasn't sending the women back and would refuse him access to Ellis. What he'd done was unforgivable, but what I would soon do was even more so.

"I don't need to eat."

I pierced him with a glare. "Please, eat and rest. Come back in three hours."

"Ellis needs me."

"Not right now, Raphael. I'm here. But he will need you soon, and so will I." The words caught in my throat like a razor.

"Why?"

I shrugged. "I have a feeling. Please. If I need you, I'll send Miles, I promise."

He left as Jessie returned the small oilcloth bag I'd requested in hand. She watched me open it and drag the contents free: the letter I'd only opened once to read and then hidden away safely.

"Miss Francesca?"

I turned and looked at her. "Have everything we need packed and transported to the dirigible. Do it carefully so nothing seems amiss. Then have the women escorted aboard in groups of two."

"But Mr Nobel doesn't know. His men will not allow—"

"Hush, Jessie. If there are questions, direct them to me."

I'd spent hours turning over the best way to get the women out of here. I was reluctant to send the message to Damien until we'd left, needing to ensure the safety of my patients first.

I looked down at the letter Adam had given me so long ago.

If at some point my son Edward chooses a path of fear and pain, you must intercede. I trust you, Francesca. You have a deep well of honesty and integrity. Those of us who abide by the rules of the Religion are legion. Not all believe. Many are like me. We are taking time and care, undoing the bonds that tie us to this way of life. We are strong. We are many.
But the teachings of lifetimes cannot be swiftly overturned, which is why I have not completed this, my life's work.
If the time comes—and in Edward, I see the unfortunate possibility—then you must invoke the Rite of Sacrifice. Raphael will know who to petition.
Above all, protect those who cannot protect themselves, Francesca.

Adam had taught me much about religion. He'd ensured I knew the finer details, all the while encouraging me to fulfil my desire to become a physiotraducere. If it hadn't been for him, I'd probably be married with a family, sewing gowns, and feeling vaguely unfulfilled.

He'd seen beneath the facade to the hunger I hid.

He'd understood my drive to help those who couldn't help themselves. Women like my long-dead mother.

"Miss Francesca?"

Jessie's query dragged me from my introspection. "Apologies, my friend."

"You're worried about something. Tell me. I can help."

I smiled and knew it was half-hearted. "On this occasion, you can't. At least not with the hard part. So, I need you to care for the women. Get them aboard quickly. I doubt we have much time, and what I'm going to do will bring more enemies down on me than friends."

"You're going to do something dangerous?"

Now there was little to do but nod.

"Why?"

"Because they need me to. The women. The children and the men without status. They cannot protect themselves, so those of us in position must attend to them. Ensure their safety. It's a responsibility I won't shirk, Jessie."

She limped over and hugged me. "You're a good woman, Francesca Hemingswood-Whitmore."

Hearing my full name melted the cold bubble inside me, and I sighed and leaned into the hug. "Thank you, Jessie. Now go. The sooner we achieve this, the sooner Miles can move Ellis and we can get out of here."

Without another word, Jessie left the room, and I slumped down into the chair. "Surely I must have been bad in a previous life to have this much trouble follow me." My gaze settled on Ellis, and wondering if I'd returned too late to save him.

* * *

Dawn was still three hours away, but when Raphael entered the room, I knew he'd caught wind of my preparations. "What the hell are you doing?" His whisper wasn't very low, and I held my hand up and ushered him from the room.

"Now, I'll explain." I moved to the door, checked the locks were firmly in place, and dragged him back to the doorway where Ellis was resting.

Miles looked up, and I nodded. With great care, he lifted the pallet we'd arranged Ellis on and placed him on the trolley.

"What are you doing?" Raphael demanded again.

"Before your father's death, Adam wrote me a letter. Do you remember the day of his burial, in the office? There was an envelope, a thick one your brother Edward handed to me. In it, there were instructions." I fished in my pocket for the package and drew it out. "Your father was worried about Edward and feared someday he'd lose sight of the community your father had agreed to protect. Adam didn't build Nobel Crest, he inherited it when it was in disarray. It wasn't always the way it was under his headship, and he worried Edward didn't have the same character to keep it on the course he'd set. He didn't want it to stay the same, though. He saw the need to one day release the bonds and was actively working on that when he passed."

"What?" He lurched closer and took the thin envelope I held in my hand. He broke the seal but didn't yet read it.

"He wanted to release the women, to ensure they were cared for, given a future. Your father wanted to disband Nobel Crest because he didn't believe in the polygamous lifestyle."

Raphael scanned the sheet of paper. "How long have you known?" His voice shook.

"He didn't tell me a lot about it. I guess it wasn't something he could discuss with a woman. It was only after I received the letter, and it was there, that I knew. He asked me not to tell you. Not until you saw the damage for yourself. He knew one day you'd come to me for assistance. It's why he encouraged my studies and my commitment to the foundation, so I'd have contacts and knowledge. They were words he used frequently."

Raphael closed his eyes, and I had the feeling he was hearing his father's words in his mind. "He did. Father always encouraged us to do and be the best we could."

I wanted to go to him in that moment, to comfort him, but I wouldn't. I didn't dare trust myself. "Edward will send men soon to subdue the women and take them back. To keep Ellis separated and to take me to task."

He agreed. It was there in his stance. "Yes. You're outside the Crest family, but he will need you to pay for the insult, real or imagined."

"Jessie was rounding the women up, getting them onto the dirigible. Miles has transported all my items and things we may need for Ellis. I can't ever return, even though I made a promise to your father. There is no longer safety for me here."

Raphael nodded, and in his eyes, I read grief. "We should leave." He held out his hand, and I took it.

The night was still, the darkness near overwhelming. We moved in silence, keeping to the edges and corners, using the deepest shadows in case someone watched. Finally we reached the dirigible and hurried up the steps.

The gangplank retracted, and we were rising into the air as the first rays of dawn peeked over the horizon. I watched as the gates of Nobel Crest opened, saw the men down below, Edward Nobel astride a large black horse leading the way.

Saw the moment he became aware we'd left, heard the echoes of shouts. Then I retreated inside at Raphael's request.

Chapter Six

On our arrival home, we climbed into the horseless carriages we'd called ahead for.

Raphael barely acknowledged me, since I'd explained what must be done.

In the lounge, far away from the others, Raphael glanced at me. "What don't I know that I must?"

I inhaled, the breath unsteady. I'd not shown him the other letter, the one that explained what he'd been doing for decades. Now I held it out. "Read this."

He scanned it, his face paling, and by the end, he was shocked to the core. "You kept this from me?"

I nodded. "As he requested."

"All these years, you took the castigation, the..."

"Because I knew, one day, you'd be ready to know the truth. Adam was a good man, Raphael. He trusted me, and I listened, learned, and made every effort to thank him for his care. The Haven clan men were evil, and I survived because of my mother, Amaryllis, and Damien. Because they saw in me something I didn't. I wanted to make them proud, so I worked hard and give everything I can back to the women who have no one to stand for them. Adam knew I'd do that."

Raphael's hand snaked out and gripped mine. At that moment, I felt a deep connection zinging between us. I didn't pull away, because right then, Raphael needed my strength, I told myself.

"You were wronged for all these years."

"Yes, but I kept my tongue for a purpose, Raphael. The same as you did when you left, didn't you? Otherwise, you wouldn't be working with Damien and the government. I know very little about the organisation, only that it exists and one day hopes to see freedom for the women."

He sighed. "A strong woman. Damien talks as if you're somehow indestructible."

I laughed at that. "Anything but. Simply driven, I think."

"Yes," he muttered. "Forgive me. All those years ago, I believed Edward. He said you expected a place at the table, money, and power. That you had designs far above any station a woman deserved."

I laughed again, then sobered. "Adam and I spent hours talking. He spoke of other cultures, other ways. He talked of rights and politics. The many ways we can all make a difference in the world. I thought we simply connected like grandfather and granddaughter." I blushed, felt the heat on my cheeks. "Preposterous though it might be, I sometimes wished he were my grandfather."

Raphael pulled his hand away, and I mourned the loss of connection, but then he cupped my cheek. "No, not preposterous at all. In you, I believe he found a kindred spirit. We used to talk too until he sent me off to see the world. I'd only just returned when he passed away."

"Yes, he missed you. Missed the closeness you shared. I think, in some small way, I filled the gap you left." The touch of his hand on my face made my insides quiver. "He was a good man, Raphael." I looked him in the eye. "Your brother was jealous. He was busy in the office, building his empire, and Adam was ill. I don't think he understood how much power your brother was wielding by that time."

"So, what do I do now?"

"You must invoke the Rite of Sacrifice. Your father said you'd know who to petition, but with that action, Nobel Crest must stand alone. It can't request assistance from other houses. We must strip his power quickly while setting in place protections for those who can't stand up for themselves."

He drew away and inhaled sharply. "But that would—"

"I know. For him, it will be unforgivable. But, Raphael, the women on board? Their stories are horrifying. He raped more than one. Beat them. Two most certainly carry children, as does a third as well, I believe. They deserve both a future and safety."

He pulled away, turned. It cut me deeply.

He'd not spoken another word to me on our journey. The chill in the air surrounded me as I sat in the carriage beside him. I might as well have been alone.

When the carriage came to a stop, I waited until he'd alighted, then climbed out. He didn't offer an arm, and I felt as if though I'd somehow insulted him. My chest ached in response.

Stepping up to the house, I reached for the door handle at the same time as Raphael. "Forgive me," he mumbled, pulling back.

I gave a sharp nod and stepped inside.

Chaos reigned, with the staff racing around. I stopped, and Raphael bumped into me.

Aloysius ran up. "Miss Francesca, there's a fire at the rear. Please, if you'd wait outside."

My senses moved to high alert. "Where? Show me." There was no way I'd allow my people to be in danger while I merely oversaw their actions.

He grimaced. "It's really best you wait outside." It wasn't panic in his voice so much as fury, and he glanced over my shoulder.

"Travis Haven?" Raphael questioned.

Aloysius grimaced. "Likely, Mr Nobel. Please, keep her out there for a little longer. The men almost have it under control." Then he melted back inside.

With firm hands, Raphael tugged me back away from the door.

"I need to see—"

"You'll only be in their way. Let them do their jobs in peace."

I opened my mouth, then closed it again, having more than once uttered something similar.

Long moments passed as the wafting scent of burning filled the air. I paced, furious with myself that I'd been so mired in my self-pity that I'd missed the sounds and smells of the fire.

Aloysius finally emerged from the building, his face sooty and mouth tight. "The fire is out, and the house is safe. Please come in now, Miss Francesca."

In silence, I trailed my father's major-domo inside, then waited for the door to shut behind me. "What happened?" I demanded.

"A delivery arrived just before you did. The maid didn't check who sent it, and it seems there was an incendiary device. The package was addressed to you, but it hadn't proceeded past the kitchen."

"And no one was injured?"

"No, Miss Francesca." He bowed his head.

At that, the adrenaline holding me up gave way, and I felt my legs turn to noodles. "Good." I reached for a chair and slid down. "What damage is there to the house itself? Will it be secure?" I vividly remembered the flight from the house as a child again.

"It's safe, Miss Francesca. Your father made alterations after you left for the islands. It's also how we contained the fire so quickly. He reinforced the structures of the exterior, and there are cog-operated fire suppression systems, cranks that pump the water through discharge nozzles on the ceiling."

"Oh. Are they installed throughout the house?"

He smiled and nodded. "Indeed they are, Miss Francesca."

Raphael cleared his throat. "I'll come have a look at the mess. I'll also talk to the maid and see if there are any clues as to what took place."

I said nothing. There didn't really seem to be much that could be said, so I stayed while Aloysius and Raphael disappeared. I hadn't slept in nearly a full day, and while the grittiness of my eyes and the ache of my body certainly clamoured at me, my brain was spinning in sharp circles of disarray.

Was I endangering the staff by remaining here? Would the clinic be next? What of the safety of my patients and staff?

My limbs tremored, and hot tears pricked at my eyelids. I bit my lip, scrunched my eyes up tight, and concentrated on my breathing. I had overcome a lot so far, and no single man would bring me down. If I had to leave to protect those close to me, I would.

Travis Haven will not win.

When Raphael returned, I had a modicum of control over my emotions.

"Francesca, you should rest."

I glanced up at him, inspecting his face, noting the shadow of dirt on one cheek. My hands itched to swipe it away. "But not here. The best thing is to leave the house. If Travis Haven can't find me—"

"He'll simply continue to attack this location now, whether or not you're here. He'll see he was successful in scaring you off if you don't remain."

The words stopped me. If he was truly fixated, then it didn't really matter what I did. And that put everything I'd worked for at risk.

"We need guards on the clinic and foundation buildings. Miles and Jessie must also be moved into the house here. I will not have them risked."

Raphael nodded. "I would agree. Anyone important to you, including all your staff here, will need to be considered. Reginald may well be safe with his grandmother, but—"

"We'll need to contact him, ensure he has adequate guards when travelling." I stood and rubbed my aching head.

"And now you need to rest, Francesca."

At his words, I spun. "Dr Whitmore," I corrected, echoing words I'd spoken mere days before.

He smiled, but it was sad. "I hurt you, and for that, I apologise."

My lips trembled. "I... No, you've just become forward in the last day or two."

He lifted his hand and cupped my cheek. "I'm truly sorry. I was lost inside the mess in my head. My brother and how he's changed, the letter from my father and the intelligence you shared." He leaned in, his breath whispering over my lips. "I wasn't doubting you, but there was much to come to terms with. My mother always said I was too deep, and when dealing with a life-changing truth, I don't talk to people."

His eyes gazed into mine, and the clarity I now saw was the complete opposite of the shut-out man from earlier in the day.

"I..." Words escaped me. What was it I even wanted to say? That I believed him, but I rejected any hope for a romantic future? That no man was trustworthy? I knew that wasn't the truth. Damien and Andrew had taught me that. As had Reginald, Aloysius, and countless others. That I didn't trust easily because of the likes of Travis Haven damaging something inside me was a truth I couldn't utter.

"You've not had an easy time. My own actions made the situation far worse, and for that, there aren't enough words to explain, but I do deeply regret them, Fran—Dr Whitmore."

It felt like he could read the fears inside my heart and mind, and I wasn't comfortable with that concept at all.

I tugged away. "I'm going upstairs. I'm going to bathe and lie down." As far as defences went, it was pretty weak but all I had.

Rising took an effort, and he watched me, then followed me up the stairs.

"What are you doing?"

"Making sure you reach your room. You're swaying with tiredness."

I opened my mouth to remonstrate, but the energy it would take to defend myself was lacking, so I concentrated on putting one foot in front of the other. At my door, I spun, and he was there, gaze watchful. His very presence was heavy and overwhelming.

I wanted so much. I needed sleep, but it was as if my brain had reached a limit of normal capacity. "I wish…"

"What do you wish?"

His voice dropped a full octave, and I felt the shock of it in my belly. "I want you to kiss me."

Raphael stilled, his mouth dropping open, and I wished I could swallow the words. I groped for the doorknob, wishing myself anywhere but here and my mouth tied shut.

"A kiss?"

"No, that's not what I meant," I babbled, feeling the heat of a deep blush on my face.

He stepped closer, and if it were possible, I was sure I could claim he swallowed the very oxygen from my lungs. "The lady demands a kiss."

"I didn't demand, I said I wish." My brain came close to exploding as I realised what I'd just said.

He moved, the action so quick I didn't see it coming, so the graze of his lips against mine startled me. My hand stopped the useless quest and hung still while my brain seized with awareness of him, his nearness, the fact that he was here. *Kissing* me, Francesca Whitmore.

When he pulled away, his eyes glittered with something I barely understood but heated me from the inside. My bones had turned to wet oatmeal. and thinking straight was a miracle I couldn't count on.

"Good night, Francesca," he whispered. "Sleep well, and dream of me." Then he winked, stepped back, and walked toward the stairs, his step jaunty.

I stood where I was, fingers touching my slightly swollen lips as I wondered how on earth I was going to get myself out of this mess. Or even, for that matter, if I really wanted to.

With no easy answer, I turned, found the dratted doorknob, and entered my bedroom.

Chapter Seven

I rose early, my sleep disappointing and disjointed. With a mutter, I lurched for the bathroom and set about my morning routine. Even as I entered my chamber, once more clean and fresh, I knew something had changed.

The gown I'd chosen for the day, a deep blue with black embroidery, waited, as did my maid, Louisa. My choice of clothing felt vaguely uninspiring. I bit my lip but allowed my maid to assist me so I dressed with speed. I'd never been one to lie abed.

Settling at my toilette table, I hastily twisted my hair, noting the curl I ruthlessly tamed, and my high winged eyebrows. I took the time to consider my visage. My lips weren't overly wide but were an acceptable shade of pink. My skin was clear, with enough natural rose to please.

My eyes were clear and fringed with long lashes.

"Miss Francesca?" Louisa caught me mid-examination, and I closed my eyes while the flush of embarrassment passed.

"Yes, thank you." I rose and made for the door, then turned back, watching for an instant as she scurried about, clearing away any untidiness I'd left behind me.

In the hallway, I soothed the jumble in my belly, smoothing down the front of the gown before inhaling and stepping once more into my daily life.

Raphael waited in the morning room, his plate filled with tasty morsels of eggs and bacon, his coffee steaming and aromatic.

"Good morning," I said, sliding into my chair, hoping to set the tone of the day. Professional, polite, yet distant.

"Francesca." He smiled.

My stomach flip-flopped at the intimacy of that single word. "I have a full list for today," I began.

He shook his head. "No you don't. Reginald has taken over the urgent cases. Jessie and Miles spoke with me, and Dr Lefevre will fill in for the rest. The foundation is self-sustaining."

"What? You rearranged my bookings, contacted my staff? You've overstepped, Raphael Nobel." Hot tears of rage burned my eyes while I scrunched the napkin in my hand.

"No, and yes. No, I haven't overstepped. Travis Haven wants to kill you, my dear. Your being in the clinic poses a greater risk to your patients and your staff. You agreed I would keep you safe. You want the clinic and staff protected? I've given orders to have men in the clinic full-time. Your staff will move onto the premises here. Where I have over-stepped is that we will leave later today. Your maid is packing a bag, and we depart in an hour."

Shock coursed through me. "Leaving?" I slumped as if the stuffing were knocked from my body. "Why? You said…"

"I know., but it's not safe. Francesca, he *will* kill you. We need to get you somewhere safe."

I bit my lip. "But if I run away, when will I ever be able to stop? I can't live my life this way, Raphael."

He stared at me, his eyes piercing. "We'll get him."

I inhaled deeply, felt my lungs gulp down the oxygen. "I've been down this road before. Ammy and Damien whisked us away, and while it removed one layer, it didn't kill the cult. The beast has many heads, Raphael."

He appeared troubled by my comment, his forehead creasing. Had I hit a nerve?

"Francesca, nothing is certain. But I will keep you safe or die trying."

I gasped. "No one dies for me, Raphael." The very thought of that… it was like being hit with a hammer blow. "No one," I reiterated.

He blinked slowly, and then a lazy smile crept over his face. "Why, Francesca, anyone would think you cared about me."

Ire rose within me, heat blasting my face. "I will not be responsible." I pushed away from the table and left the room, the sound of quiet laughter echoing in my wake.

In the hallway, I stilled, trying desperately to recompose myself.

"Miss? I have a letter for you." A housemaid extended the small, folded missive, and I accepted it with a smile I had to force.

I broke the seal.

What a shame, Francesca. Yes, I know who you are. I know every-thing. Your mother died a long, slow death, and that bitch Amaryllis betrayed us all, then adopted you. One act is all it took, and now you wear a target.
Tell me, have they started the repairs on your house yet?
One day, you will pay the price I demand. No one crosses Travis Haven.
Haven House will rise again.
TH

The scrawl was spidery, but it was the sheer malice of the words that froze me where I stood.

"Miss? Will there be a response, miss?" The words were rote. She'd asked this question so many times in the past, it seemed like they were automatic.

I shook my head and slid the letter into my pocket. "No." She turned. "Wait. Who delivered this?"

She shrugged. "The footman said it came by courier, Miss Francesca."

"Did he wait?"

The girl shook her head. "I don't think so."

Yet another dead end. "Thank you," I whispered and watched her retreat.

I should tell Raphael. I didn't want to, though. It would strengthen his claim, but in the cold reality of daylight, I considered what he'd told me. The weight of his pronouncement that, by remaining, I put everyone else in danger. That couldn't be ignored.

I wouldn't tolerate causing harm. It was counter to everything I'd agreed to when I'd become a physiotraducere. Protect and enhance life. That was my personal mission.

Biting my lip, I returned to the dining room.

Raphael looked up. "Everything all right?"

Can he read on my face the battle I'm dealing with? "I'm fine," I answered and tried to keep my face a neutral mask. "You're right, and I'm acting foolish. Where are we going?"

He shook his head. "I'll explain once we're on the way."

I detested being in the dark about my life, but I understood that right now, power wasn't mine to wield. I'd simply have to bide my time.

* * *

The carriage rumbled to a stop, and I looked outside. "We aren't at the main terminal."

"No. We're taking something smaller, meeting another conveyance, and then..." He shrugged, eyes shadowed in the depths of the carriage. "I promise I'll reveal all soon."

The door opened, and he moved out, then reached for and took my hand. A small hot air balloon waited at the edge of a field, striped in yellow, red, and blue. The basket was large enough for us and the two bags and single trunk we carried. Perhaps my maid had packed too much, the journal I'd insisted on and the physiological texts additional weight. "I've brought too much."

He shook his head. "No, it'll be fine." The two burly men who had travelled with us carted the bags and case over, settling them inside the capacious basket, and Raphael urged me forward.

"I've never travelled this way before," I muttered as Raphael assisted me into my coat that he'd insisted I'd need. "You said it'll be cool in the air?"

He nodded, eyes on the road we'd traversed. "Yes," His short answer surprised me. "We should go." He followed me in, waited as the pilot or balloonsman—what was the correct term?—fastened the small gate and nodded to those waiting nearby. They thrust ropes into the basket around us. "You should sit down," Raphael added.

Not that I wanted to, but I was in his hands, and the frown on his face was deepening, so I did as he commanded.

Inside my belly, a knot was forming. One built of terror. Had someone followed us? I would ask when he was less tense.

The balloon rose, slowly at first, then with more speed as Raphael muttered to the man in charge. Large bursts of noise came from the burner below the balloon, intriguing because I'd never seen the like before. I concentrated on it, watching every action and attempting to deduce what they did.

Several minutes passed before Raphael's body seemed to unclench. "You can look now."

I rose tentatively and moved to the edge of the basket, gripping it tight as I glanced over the side.

"Did someone follow us?"

He tensed beside me, hands clenched on the wicker, knuckles white. "Yes. My men are of the opinion that Travis was watching and waiting."

The paper in my pocket burned through layers of fabric. *I should tell him. Perhaps when we reach our destination?*

"Where are we going, Raphael?'

He sighed. "My mother came from a small cattle ranch. East of here but too far to reach by balloon. We're travelling to Caltenville and will meet a small dirigible there."

"You arranged another private—"

"It helps that I own the company, Francesca."

Of course. The men of the cults, particularly those in high positions or families of the highly placed, were always assisted to build empires. Meanwhile, the women were little more than breeders and cleaners.

I turned away, not wanting him to see the fury that must surely have been evident on my face.

"Francesca?"

He touched my shoulder, and I stiffened. I wanted to shrug it away, but the training of a dozen years dictated I not act so rudely. Hot tears pricked my eyelids.

"I'm not like the others, Francesca," he whispered against my ear. "I will take a wife in due course. *A* wife. One."

The words startled me, and I began to turn, but his hand held me in place. I got the impression that he wanted to say more, but we started descending, slowly floating downward like a feather on the wind.

When the basket touched the ground, I could see a small dirigible waiting across the paddock. Sleek and coppery in colour, it glinted in the sunlight. Large screws attached to blades which would propel us, and above, the inflatable balloon that would carry us once more aloft but with speed.

On the side, the large nameplate gleamed. The *Lady Anthea*. I knew that name. "Your mother?"

He nodded. "She was truly a lady, born and bred. My father adored her, but he was forced to take more wives. She was the only bride he had multiple children with."

I bit my lip. "Why?"

He grimaced. "Once we reach home." My eyes must have widened at his use of the word "home," because he sighed. "It's a very long story, Francesca. And not one for here."

He hustled me from the basket, and I stepped onto deep grass, watching as several men stamped toward us. He didn't introduce me, merely gave a stern order for them to retrieve our items and be quick. Without another word, his hand found its place at the small of my back, and he propelled me toward the ship.

We made our way up the extendible ramp and on board. Here I was stunned. Where the dirigibles I'd travelled on before were utilitarian with a private lounge, everything about this one oozed prosperity and comfort. Luxury.

Carpets were laid down for us to walk upon, and once inside, the scent of wooden polish—with a hint of beeswax, I detected—the highly polished gold door fittings, and the brocade and dark wood furnishings astounded me. Lights were lit in the glass fittings adorning the hallway, and he led me to the first door. Inside was a small dining area, set with table and chairs, a white lacy tablecloth, and dark red curtains and carpets.

"Well..." I was lost for words.

"My mother collected all these furnishings, and when she passed, my father knew I'd want them. He kept them for me at the ranch. When the time came for the *Lady Anthea* to be launched, this is what I wanted. Would you like something to eat, to rest, or shall I show you the rest of the ship?"

Anticipation bubbled inside me. "I'd really like to look around."

Raphael grinned at my enthusiasm, and once more he indicated that we should traverse down the hall. "There are four sleeping chambers on this deck. These are for family and friends. The crew are all comfortably accommodated below on the two staffing decks."

I blinked. "How many levels are there?"

"Four. One is for cargo, supplies, and the engine bay and mechanical workshop. Then two layers of staffing decks, and then this. There is a cockpit to the bow as well, but I don't wish to bother the captain. He and his first mate will be busy for the next two days."

I frowned. "That long?"

"Yes. We'll make landfall tonight and rest, then set off again early in the morning. This craft isn't built for overnight flights. As you probably deduced, it's for pleasure trips, and while quick, it can still only cover forty-three knots per hour."

I gasped. "Why, that's..." Surely nothing else could move at those speeds? "Is it safe?"

Raphael laughed. "Yes. Her top speed is in the range of fifty-five knots, but I don't like to push her so fast. We'll travel the first 600 miles today, then finish the journey tomorrow at around 670 miles. The ship will house us for the period we're travelling, though, and will take on fuel overnight."

Stopping at the next door, he opened it to show me a lush bedroom, of gold and green. I stepped inside, moving my head from side to side as I took in all the sights. "This bed," I murmured, sliding my hand over the soft counterpane.

"Every chamber has a private bathing room. Small and practical." He opened the door with a flick of the wrist, and I glanced within. A white porcelain water-chair, sink with faucet, and a small hip bath. The room itself shone as the light above the small pedestal vanity unit gleamed.

"Come," he urged, and I followed like a child.

Each room was more magnificent than the last until the final chamber.

"This is my room," he intoned.

Unlike the others, the dark blue was accented with silver. The window coverings were pulled aside, and I noted the metal of the bed was black, fading it from sight. The room was more relaxed than the other chambers, with a large chair sitting near a desk covered in detritus. The bathing room showed signs of his previous occupation too, with shelves beside the mirror, each surrounded by a lip so nothing would fall.

A painting sat by the door, a woman in clothing some ten to fifteen years out of date. Her features were fine, her hair dressed in a style no longer favoured except by the matrons of society. Around her neck sat a pearl and enamelled choker. Matching bobs hung from her ears. But it was the piercing gaze of grey-green that captured my attention. Raphael's eyes.

"Your mother," I stated.

"Yes. She was born Lady Anthea. Her father and mother had emigrated from England not long after her birth. All my grandparents' other children died on the voyage or not long before, and she was coddled and adored. Her education surpassed that of many statesmen."

I waited for more, but he wasn't forthcoming. I turned away and headed back into the hallway. "Which chamber would you prefer I used?"

"The gold chamber."

The one next to his. For a moment, blood pounded in my veins as our gazes locked.

"Raphael..." My voice took on a breathless quality, and I could have sworn an invisible thread tugged us together. I felt myself sway, mesmerised by the flare of deep emotion in his eyes, until the rattle of feet on the deck snapped the connection.

I backed away, one step and then another, my face burning. I lifted my hands, cupped my cheeks.

"Where would you like the lady's things, Master Raphael?"

He gave instructions while I waited, uncomfortably aware that I'd almost committed to something I didn't want to understand.

When the men departed, I ducked my head. "I might have a lie-down," I mumbled and then ducked into the room, shutting the door and leaning against it, eyes squeezed shut. *What am I doing?* I couldn't believe I'd almost kissed him. Raphael Nobel. Scion of the house of Nobel. Brother of the master of Nobel Crest —a cultist and potential bigamist to boot.

He says he only wants one wife, my brain whispered.

"Clearly his father said that too," I muttered. "Doesn't mean he won't if necessary."

The racing of my heart reminded me that everything I told myself was a lie. I wanted to believe those words. Wanted to fall into the deep wells of promise in his eyes. Wanted that taste. That touch.

"No," I remonstrated with myself, tugging away from the door and stalking to the bathroom. Splashing my face with water, I felt the lift, heard the engines whining, and knew we'd started the steady climb into the heavens.

I could hide in here, claim exhaustion from the travelling and the worry, but I wasn't a weakling or one prone to fits of sulking. With a last look at myself in the mirror and an adjustment of my hat, I inhaled deeply, felt my lungs filling with oxygen.

"I will go out there. Nothing will distress me. I will meet his gaze and be self-assured."

Chapter Eight

Dinner that night was served in the dining room. The candles were lit as we travelled through the gloom. "It's easier to have them finalise the cooking before we begin the ascent. If the landing is heavy for some reason, we run the risk of spillage, loss, and fire," Raphael explained.

I nodded and spooned my soup up. It was delightful, the creamy mushroom full-bodied. "Your staff are well trained."

He smiled, though there was a touch of strain around his mouth. "Yes. Just because it's only meant to carry a small number of guests doesn't mean they shouldn't give quality service. I believe Cook has something special planned for the main course, isn't that right, Jenkins?"

The man, dressed in severe black, the white of his shirt and gloves immaculate, nodded. "Yes, sir. Duck a la fricassee, I believe."

I glanced up with surprise. "But that takes nearly two days!"

"Cook started the preparations as soon as Master Raphael sent instructions. Especially when we heard he was bringing a lady aboard."

I raised an eyebrow at that but kept my silence. After all, if he regularly brought women aboard for the purposes of surprising and wooing them, it was none of my business. It wasn't as if—

I cut off the thought, not wanting to dwell any further on it.

Raphael cleared his throat. "What Jenkins means is I rarely have ladies aboard. Usually they're a half-sister being transported with their husband somewhere, or otherwise friends. I don't bring—" He scowled.

"You don't bring what, exactly?" My tone was harsh, and he winced.

"I'm not in the habit of being around unaccompanied women," he muttered.

"Oh." Where did I go with that? Surely he had paramours, as did most of the men before they settled on a first, second, and even third wife. It had been the way of the men of Haven, and of Nobel too, from what I'd gleaned. Why was Raphael different?

Jenkins collected the dishes after we finished the soup course in silence, and for a short while, the room was empty except for Raphael and me.

"Francesca, earlier I tried to tell you about my thoughts. I want—"

The door slid open, and Jenkins returned with a large silver platter and two domed plates. Raphael closed his mouth.

I found myself wanting to ask him what he'd been about to say, yet the silence was telling. Whatever it was, he felt strongly enough that it was private so as not to speak of it in front of Jenkins.

Strange and telling, I thought.

Jenkins laid out the plates, and I glanced down, the duck pieces perfect, the scent of orange wafting up from the table. I started to eat, giving the plate my whole attention, well aware that Jenkins hovered, wine bottle now in hand, ready to top up our glasses.

Once the plate was empty, I smiled. "That was truly a highlight of the evening." Then I faked a yawn behind my hand. Staying here longer, keeping sweet while confusion roared through my veins, wasn't the way I intended to spend the evening. I had reading I could complete, or I could sleep, a commodity that was far scarcer than in my pre-physiotraducere days. If I was "running" from truths I didn't want to explore, then so be it. I'd learned in my life that sometimes remaining uninvolved was the safest option.

"If you'll forgive me, Raphael, I find myself suddenly fatigued. I believe I will retire."

Across the table, his smooth forehead took on a frown, "But, Francesca—"

I rose, sliding my napkin to the table. With a quiet "Thank you" to Jenkins, I escaped down the hall to my chamber.

* * *

We finally arrived at the ranch late the following evening. We'd been travelling for some time over rocky but clearly heavily cultivated terrain when the building came into view, and the *Lady Anthea* settled at the transportation station.

I'd taken great care in the last eighteen hours to keep conversations light and impersonal, book always in hand, to ward off the discussions of emotions and anything that might discommode me.

Now, as I made my way down the gangplank, I looked around. It was remote and yet majestic in ruggedness. Large trees fringed the house, though it was no farmhouse but rather a sprawling building of stone with ramparts and formal gardens.

"This is your family's home?"

"My home. My grandfather carved up his holdings. The investments went to my older brother, the seafaring interests to the younger, and I inherited the estate, all the equipment, and so on."

"How much land?" I enquired.

"Just over four thousand acres."

So much land. I could barely contemplate the size of it. That would mean everything I could see belonged to Raphael.

"Travis Haven would find it hard to track you down here. I thought it might give us time to tease out what he's been doing, where he's hiding, and maybe even find whoever is backing him, since the Haven properties were seized after the attack on Amaryllis and Damien."

The words had me twisting in his direction. "Just how long do you plan to stay here?" I narrowed my eyes while a pit in my stomach yawed.

He shrugged, avoiding my gaze. "As long as is necessary."

"Dammit, Raphael. I can't stay here forever... or even indefinitely. I have responsibilities. A life. Friends."

"Yes, you have a life. One he'd snuff out in an instant because he's unstable, Francesca." The ice in his tone should have chilled me to the bone, but it didn't. Instead, it fanned the rage building inside me.

"You have no right—"

He reached out toward me, but didn't touch as if he was concerned how I'd react. "I do, Francesca. Believe me, I want nothing more than your prickly tongue to—"

"Stop it, Raphael. I'm not one of the many women who can be cajoled or beguiled by a glib tongue and promises of comfort all my life. I'm an independent woman. An educated person. A physiotraducere, so don't think I'll fall for this."

His gaze narrowed, his lips taking on white bracketing, and he straightened up under my onslaught. "Well, that tells me where I stand, I guess."

"It does," I bit out. "Now, are we going to stand out here all day, or shall we proceed inside?"

He waved me forward, and I marched, suddenly and inexplicably deflated now that the flash of rage was passing.

The double doors opened as I reached the first step, and a liveried footman stepped outside. "Welcome home, sir. And Dr Whitmore, welcome to Carlington House. It's an honour to have you join us."

Those kind words of welcome shamed me as much as the memory of the scorn I'd just thrown at Raphael. *I'll need to make amends,* I told myself and then stepped inside the gracious mansion.

My coat was deftly removed and spirited away, and I was ushered into the family parlour, as the footman called it. Once settled on a deeply cushioned settee, I waited for Raphael, who slowly ambled in.

"Welcome to my home," he muttered.

"Raphael, I'm sorry."

"Don't be, Dr Whitmore. Now I understand I'm here solely to protect your life and liberty. We're all—"

I rose and stalked forward. "Please, Raphael," I beseeched, but ice glittered in his eyes, goading me.

"Doctor, I believe the evening meal will be ready shortly. You can either wait here or—"

Some devilry must have urged my actions, as I caught his hand and tugged him forward before rising on my toes and stopping him, our faces inches apart. "Raphael," I whispered.

"Don't, Francesca. Don't offer me crumbs."

I waited just a second too long, because arms slid around my waist and closed the distance between us. His lips, firm and hungry, found mine.

Time ceased.

It must have, because how else could I describe the way I noted every inch of his body, plastered against mine, every hard and rigid muscle? How else could I explain the way his kiss tasted of coffee, tobacco, and sin? Or the way pleasurable zings of energy seemed to enter my body and demand more from me than I'd previously known?

His hands slid down, one firmly gripping my hip and anchoring me while the other crept up to the nape of my neck, caressing and promising things I barely understood but so desperately wanted to explore.

The touch of his skin against the exposed flesh of my neck had me arching, demanding more without a word.

It was a surprise, then, when he released me. I was left dazed and at sea, confused because I wanted more but felt indignation at the liberties he'd taken with my person. I stepped away, invisibly tugging my cloak of dignity around myself. "I... That was quite a..."

His mouth curled in derision, and I couldn't tell if it was at me or himself. Either notion pierced me. "I will return soon. If you need anything, ring the bell. One of the maids will collect you for dinner, or you can request that they escort you to your chamber."

He turned and left me, and I felt cold and miserable. I'd gone from yelling at him to almost climbing atop him, then allowed—enjoyed— the intimacy of his kiss.

Biting my lip, I turned away, pacing the floor for long moments. I was no tease. I didn't behave like this.

"I won't allow myself to turn into a screaming shrew," I lectured myself. "Nor am I missish. I'm a woman of destiny and means with many depending on me, not just for their livelihoods but also their lives." Assured I'd regained a firm grip on myself, I reached for the bell pull and waited for one of the maids to arrive. "If I could please be directed to my chamber? I'd appreciate the chance to clean up a little."

"Of course, Doctor. Mr Jones, the footman, told us you'd arrived. He said you're a doctor from the city. My brother Danny would surely appreciate your visit. He was kicked by a horse several years ago and refused anything more than the local doctor, but if you could spare the time?"

The girl chattered on, and I agreed that I'd make the time to visit with her brother and the others of the region in need of medical assistance. By the time I'd reached my room, Jenny, as she'd introduced herself, had told me she'd been here since "Master Raphael's" grandparents had passed, working up from scullery maid to now senior housemaid.

"Of course, when Her Ladyship passed, His Lordship declined quickly. He missed his daughter, Miss Anthea, sorely. She'd been the only child to survive the journey, and his parents had seen the earlier children perish in the cold winters. Her death was a severe blow to them both."

She opened the door to the chamber, and my breath caught in my throat. "Master Raphael was insistent you should have Miss Anthea's room. It's bright and beautifully appointed. The furnishings were imported from France for her, and the bedspread was embroidered by Her Ladyship."

She indicated to the door beside the fireplace. "This bathroom has a fireplace too. There's running water, both hot and cold, should you wish to bathe, and Leona, Miss Anthea's personal maid's daughter, will be happy to assist you. She was sent to London to train and returned only two months ago. Master Raphael insisted she should take time with her parents before he'd assist her in finding a position."

Every word she uttered was like a spike in my heart. Had I been too vicious with my anger? It seemed as if he'd not just given these people employment but also a purpose and lifestyle many others would only aspire to. All without needing to take multiple wives.

The question teetered on the tip of my tongue, but I held it back, refusing to reveal my own inner turmoil.

"This is lovely, Jenny. Master Raphael was very kind making the room available to me." I meant the words, truly.

* * *

I waited in the dining room, the long table between us almost anticlimactic. I needed to apologise for my behaviour. The unpleasantries I'd flung at him burned me like bile.

Several staff circled the table, serving us with the exquisite dishes prepared by his chef, as the tickle of bubbles from fine French champagne exploded on my tongue. If we were alone...

You're not, my mind added.

So, I ate and answered the questions he'd asked. Was my room comfortable? Would Leona be acceptable?

After the meal, we rose together. He took my hand, though the barely there touch reminded me of the offense I'd caused, and we proceeded to the drawing room.

I took the seat offered, and he settled himself opposite me. The chill in the air had nothing to do with the nip of the season but more to do with the accusations I'd flung.

Once we had drinks and the staff withdrew, I reached out and touched his hand. "Raphael, I'm so sorry. I spoke without thought or consideration."

"But they were honest words."

"Perhaps they were, but when spoken in the heat of anger, they were thoughtless. Careless and hurtful. For that, I apologise."

His eyes glinted, and I knew I'd injured him with my barbs. I could only hope he could forgive me.

"I was angry, affronted, and I don't like being handled. I spent my entire life prior to Amaryllis and Damien at the beck and call of men. After my birth father died, my mother was given to another. He was a..." I rubbed my stomach, because the words I was about to speak still had the power to wound me. Deeply. "He was evil. At night, once he'd finished with my mother, he'd enter my bedroom." I twisted my hands in my lap and looked down at them, more than slightly aware that what I said next might give him an utter distaste of me. "He... he would stand there, naked, Raphael. Touching himself. It sickened me, because I know what he was thinking." I gulped down the bile that rose, coating my tongue and souring my stomach. "You couldn't live in that environment and not know what he planned. When he died, I was thankful, until the reality of our situation became apparent. My mother was ill, and I cared for her, educated the children, and hoped something would change. It did, but only because my mother died."

"God damn that bastard, Francesca." He slid from his seat and onto his knees before me, taking my ice-cold hand in his. "You say he didn't touch you. You tell the truth?" His eyes bored into me, as if checking to ensure I had.

"Yes, Raphael. He didn't defile me. I was still too young at his death for even that to be allowed."

I felt him trembling and glanced up. Banked fury lived in his eyes. Hot. Enraged.

"No man should ever inflict that on a child. Every child should be sacred."

The words spewed forth, as if the act had just taken place in his mind. How did I make him realise that all those years ago, it had forged the steely intent I had absorbed into myself? "It was a long time ago. I learned and grew, let it bolster me in ways no one else would ever understand except me. But I've healed too. I know this behaviour isn't normal. It could have made me scared of men, damaged me. I haven't let that happen, Raphael. I've used it, honed myself."

"It's why you don't trust men." He ground the words out as if they carried a bitter taste.

"Not at all! I do trust men. I just choose to be wary, and my trust has to be earned." His statement had stung, and I needed to ensure he understood how my mind worked. "I won't let it determine the way I live my life, but I will use it."

"You say so now. But you're closed off toward men other than those who've been in your life for years."

I couldn't argue with that, so I watched him with wariness. *Where is this going?*

"Francesca, when you were at Nobel Crest, I wronged you. We both did." He stood now, then turned in a wide and agitated circle. "Edward led me to believe you had somehow managed to convince our father that you had plans much greater than you could achieve. That he'd been hoodwinked, and you really just wanted the money and power." This time the look he slanted at me was more than simply apologetic. It was remorseful. "I allowed him to colour my perceptions of you unfairly. I—"

I stood, amazed at the words he was speaking. For years I'd held their assessment of myself, the one where they clearly thought I was a gold digger, close to me. Now, this apology. "I... I never lied, Raphael." It seemed a banal statement, yet what more could I say? The thing was, I was overjoyed that he'd seen the truth. But now it blasted a huge hole in the wall I'd erected between us. What with that, and the kiss...

Panic swirled within me. "I... I'm going to retire." I scurried across the room, dragged the door open, and was back hiding in my chamber within moments. If only escaping my confusion was that simple. I yanked at my clothes, letting them fall to the floor. I'd already excused Leona for the night, but she'd unpacked my trunk, and night-rail waited for me on the bed. I dragged it over my body, then tugged the wrapper over my gown. Then I settled myself at the dressing table and released the pins from my hair.

For the first time, I wondered what Raphael would see if he watched my nightly preparations. Would he see a woman ripe for love or the girl he'd once known and treated shabbily?

My hands shook as I took up the brush and began the ritual, using long, steady strokes while I watched in the mirror.

The knock at the door caught me by surprise, and I surged up, brush still in my hand as I opened the door.

A tense Raphael stared at me.

"Is something wrong? Do you need my assistance? I brought my medical kit," I babbled, attempting to hide my confusion.

"I... You left so quickly that I didn't have time to tell you everything I'd wanted to say." He reached out, took my hand, and I stepped closer.

"What?"

"You're a beautiful woman, Francesca. Strong and capable. Yes, educated too, but more than that, with all the obstacles you've overcome, you've retained a softness. I wanted to tell you that these are qualities I admire greatly."

My eyes burned. "Thank you, Raphael. That means a great deal to me."

His gaze felt like it singed my skin. My body warmed as unfamiliar sensations zinged through my body. I knew from a purely academic point that it was arousal, but it was new and oh so very drugging.

"Francesca, I'm sorry. I shouldn't have barged in. It's not seemly." His cheeks shone with a ruddy glow.

Unable to help myself, I slid a fingertip over his cheek. "No, probably not." Strangely, in that short time I'd been by myself, an integral part of my mind had clarified and come to terms with what had happened before. "I don't care," she whispered.

His eyes widened. "Francesca..."

There was a warning in his tone, but instead of being alarmed, I smiled. "Raphael, you're a handsome man."

I glided my hand down his face, and I noted the rasp of evening growth.

He growled, "You're playing with fire, Francesca."

"Will it burn me?" I queried.

He swooped in then, dragging my body against his, and with few layers between our bodies, the heat of him scorched me.

The whisper of his breath caressed my face. "It'll burn us both, Francesca."

As far as warnings went, it barely had an impact; having thrown caution to the wind, I wanted whatever it was he offered.

"Raphael, ask me."

His eyes closed, and I watched his Adam's apple bob up and down. "A man can only take so much, and my restraint is limited, Francesca."

A seed of devilry pushed me further along the road of no return. "I don't want restraint, Raphael. I want fire and passion. Can you give them to me?"

He groaned, and our mouths crashed together as he pulled me close. My body tingled, the hard planes of Raphael now mashed against me.

With finesse, he deepened the connection, his mouth opening over mine, and my body sang. When his tongue surged within my mouth, I slid my own against it, glorying in the taste of him.

His hands roamed over my body, the two light layers of fine muslin no impediment to his quest, and I encouraged it, leaning back.

Our feet moved as he urged me backward until I felt the edge of my bed behind my knees, and I slumped down.

My body was starved of oxygen as we parted. On his face, there was need etched into his granite features. "If we go any further, Francesca, there will be no going back."

"I don't want to go back."

"Then you will marry me."

His words struck me like frigid water on a midwinter morning. "Marriage? I don't believe that was discussed nor agreed to," I muttered, now incensed.

Raphael's gaze narrowed. "We do this, you marry me. I won't settle for less."

"No," I said firmly. "I'm not intending to marry."

Shock was followed by fury. "I don't play, Francesca. Either you agree to become my bride, or I walk away."

He means it, I thought. "No. Why should you do that? I'm willing to allow the liberties—"

"But I will not take them, Francesca. All or nothing."

I shook my head.

He stepped back, and cold air washed over me. I didn't want him to leave. Didn't wish to be left here alone with my thoughts.

"Goodnight," he said with a formality that chilled me to the bones, then walked through the door. It shut behind him, quietly but with intent, while I sat there, shocked and confused.

"Well," I muttered and considered that I'd be spending the night alone.

Just as I had for many years.

I crawled into bed, but sleep took a long time to find me.

Chapter Nine

Morning came swiftly, but the day would stretch out before me. I took my time rising, Leona coming in sometime around nine in the morning, a cup of chocolate in her hand and a smile on her face.

"Morning, Miss Francesca. Master Raphael asked me to inform you that he'd be out today. He's visiting with the foremen and may not return until late."

That was just fine with me. After last night, I wasn't sure I intended to spend any more time in his sphere than I had to.

I bathed and dressed. Leona knew her craft well and set about arranging my hair in what she assured me was the latest style in London. "The ladies are wearing tighter corsets now, the gowns fitted at waist and bodice, Miss Francesca. Hair is almost always arranged so, with a pretty bonnet set on top. For the evenings, ruffles are *de rigeur*, and the waltz is all the rage too."

Her chatter washed over me as I prepared for the day. I meant to study the latest journal cover to cover. Physiotraducere was now an integral form of medicine, but new techniques were being trialled, and I planned to use this time to learn as much as I could.

When the call came out that an accident had occurred, I lifted my skirts and followed the men out to the field, where they'd erected temporary yards. A man rolled on the ground, hands clutching his leg. Blood pooled beneath him.

I grabbed the arm of the nearest man. "Send Leona to my chambers. Tell her the large black bag is required."

When he simply stared, I let the full force of the doctor inside me loose. "Make haste, lest the man before us perish."

I clambered through the rails, aware of the hurry to usher the cattle back to another yard, and I crouched down. "I'm a doctor. I'll help you." With a quick jerk, I grabbed both sides of the leg of his trousers and yanked, the sound of tearing fabric filling my ears. Glancing down, I immediately knew how bad the injury was.

"I need somewhere to work. A table would be best. For now, we need to control the bleeding. Then we need to move him. Quickly."

I hurried about my task, knowing exactly what needed to be done while aware of the audience gathered around me.

Leona came pelting out, and the bag was brought to me just as I finished getting a bandage of sorts onto the wound. Men moved in then, reaching down and lifting their injured comrade.

I turned to Leona. "I need an apron, something large. I'll also need water, soap, and alcohol, whatever you can find." I scurried behind the parade, my bag heavy and bouncing against my leg.

We stepped inside the barn. When I made to remonstrate, a door opened to a clean room. Already someone was washing the table down, and I held my breath.

"The veterinarian always demands a clean area. I guessed you'd want the same," a crusty older man offered.

"Indeed. Now, I must wash my hands and prepare my tools. I need someone to assist."

"Then you'd be wanting me," he offered.

A large steaming bowl of water was brought in, along with soap and a towel. I washed as best I could, then considered what I'd be doing without my usual tools, set-up, or trained assistants.

Touch-and-go, I thought, then shook it off. It wouldn't help my patient.

I took the scissors and cut away the leg of his pants, then sighed, even as the man thrashed on the table. I began with cleansing the area of the injury so I could get a better idea, thankful that my assistant held him still enough that I wouldn't take an injury to myself in the act of healing him. The injury was bad, with bone and muscle compromised. I might be able to save the limb, but he would need careful nursing under those circumstances. "Is there anyone with medical training hereabouts?"

"Not sure you can fix him?" the man beside me asked with fury in his every word.

"No," I answered carefully, "but it will make a difference to whether I can save his leg or not. If I don't amputate, he's going to need a nurse with him. We need to watch for sepsis and fever."

The man shrugged. "Only me hereabouts. I help the veterinarian when he's needed. He trained me on watching for smell, colour, and such."

It wasn't nearly enough, but I was also aware that without his leg, this man would likely starve if there was no one to care for him. I'd have to check several times a day once the initial surgery was completed. I made a decision to do my best and leaned over. "Then we begin." I sent him to my bag. "Find the bottle of chloroform. We need to knock him out."

He did, and I watched and explained how much of the liquid was needed. We waited only long enough for the man to still and close his eyes as the coppery tang of blood filled my nostrils and ran down the table leg.

I worked with care, every step methodical, stopping only now and again to stretch my back and swivel my shoulders. When I was done, I slumped into the chair in the corner, exhausted and totally unsure of the outcome in the makeshift theatre.

"Now what?" my assistant enquired.

"I wash up, and we wait. And watch." I'd done everything I could to minimise the chance of infection, but who knew?

* * *

Night had fallen by the time I left the tiny room and trudged over to the house.

Hoofbeats echoed in the night air, and I glanced up, barely having the energy to check. A man atop a large black stallion entered the yard. Raphael.

He pulled his horse up sharply, flung himself from the saddle. "Francesca?" Terror laced his words, and he grabbed me, dragged me close, his hands roaming over my body with wild moves.

"I'm quite well, thank you," I muttered.

"But... the blood." He blinked.

"Not mine. One of your men was kicked into the rails by a bull. Nearly lost his leg after it caught in a mechanism." I shrugged. "I wasn't planning on sitting around letting him bleed out or lose his leg if I could help it."

"And he's...?"

"Should live. I've left him in good care. Now, I'd really like to bathe, eat, and go to bed." I marched by him, but he reached out and grabbed my arm.

"We need to talk."

I laughed, harsh and low. "We tried that last night, remember?"

Chapter Ten

The days passed slowly. I watched my patient with concern, but his recovery, while slow, was well under way. I read from the journal I'd brought with me and kept my promise to meet with the ill and infirm of the area.

All the while, inside me, the bubble of anxiety and frustration grew larger and more pronounced.

Raphael kept away as much as he could. Mealtimes became fractious affairs, and I ate little in his presence, instead focusing on myself, my emotions ruthlessly controlled.

It was only a matter of time.

Chapter Eleven

Crossing the hall, my feet beat a rapid tattoo. Breakfast had been solitary, something I'd made a study of, so I saw Raphael as little as possible, but slothful rest wasn't something I could clearly handle with either aplomb or comfort.

I'd finished the journal, attended the numerous patients, and made suggestions, correcting what I could and referring those who needed a specialist's attention. The past two days had passed in quiet and incredibly boring communion with nature.

The heavy door squeaked as I opened it. I stomped into the library, aware that something had to change concerning my situation. Two long weeks with no movement had me climbing the walls.

"I have to go home, Raphael." My bold announcement was met with a frown and him rising from his seat. He closed the book he'd been perusing with a thud.

"Francesca, it's a pleasant surprise to see you here." The sarcastic words flowed over me.

Fury stretched its tentacles inside me at the tone. *Pleasant surprise, indeed!* I clamped down on the instinctive rejoinder, settling instead for a more mild statement. "Unless you can tell me of some action by Travis Haven against me, the clinic, or anything associated with me, I intend to return home. Tomorrow."

I gave a half nod of satisfaction. I'd come, said my piece, and would leave. I spun on the ball of my foot, but the sound of him moving and the touch of his hand on my arm stopped me. "He's tried to get to your staff."

The words knocked the stuffing out of me. I whirled back, heart pounding in my chest. "What? Are they safe?"

He gave a short nod. "I received a Marconi this morning." With a heavy sigh, he reached out across the desk, grabbed a long paper tape, and passed it to me.

Attack on house yesterday. Miles received slight injury. Guards prepared and offered resistance. First real attempt, though other testing incursions almost daily. Await instructions.

My hand reached for and found the back of a seat, and I blindly pulled myself over to it, slumping down in it. "Why? Why would he attack my people?" But I knew the truth. If he couldn't get to me, then this was the only other option.

Hiding out doesn't fix anything. It just means he has to find others, innocents to attack until I make an appearance.

I dashed at the tears that had leaked down my cheeks and straightened myself up. "This isn't right. I shouldn't be hiding here while my people are in danger." I glared at Raphael, but his face was firm, jaw tight and his eyes taking on an icy tinge.

"It's far too dangerous. We need to draw him out."

"Then let me," I cried. "My people shouldn't be endangered while I hide away like some weak little miss. I'm strong enough to do this."

He grabbed hold of me and hauled me from the chair. "He will kill you if he gets his hands on you, Francesca. I can't let that happen." His whole body radiated his fury in ways I couldn't miss.

"No, Raphael. My people need me. I intend to leave in the morning."

"Stupid woman!" he roared, tugging me closer. "Don't you see? I may not be able to save you."

"Why?" I threw at him. "Why would that cause you problems?"

"Because I care, damn it! I was wrong about you. Since Damien called me in as your bodyguard, I've seen the woman you hide. The one who gives without thought of herself. The one committed to others. She's too important. *You're* too important."

The words stopped me short. His agitation. My concerns. They all segued into a morass of need. I rose suddenly and kissed him on the mouth, remembering that one burning night when I'd learned about the intimacy of the act but lost the fragile hope I never dared allow to bloom.

My mouth opened over his while his fingers shook as they brought me closer to him. My body flamed, breasts and loins aching to know more of the sensual pleasures that had been hinted at that night.

I slid my hands within his jacket, firming over the fine shirt and tracing along his musculature. He was hard and firm and so damned enticing.

My eyes closed, and I dropped into the well of pleasure, of sights and sounds and tastes.

My tongue speared into his mouth, dancing with his until he took control, turning us so my backside crashed against his desk. I arched back, tearing my mouth from his, because it was what my body demanded.

His lips grazed my jawline, and breathing was almost impossible. One hand came up, cupping my breast over my clothing, scorching me through the layers.

"Francesca, say yes," he pleaded, his breath fanning my skin and sending lightning arcing through my body.

"I... Oh, Raphael..." The words, almost incoherent, slid between my lips as he traced the line of my neck, my body now acting on instinct, demanding and taking what it desired.

"Yes," he whispered, urging me on, hands rubbing and exploring. Thinking became something other people did; my mind whirred with erotic hunger, my body yearning for more.

"I... *Yesssssss*...," I groaned, not caring what I agreed to.

"Mine," he muttered and swooped in again, the kiss bruising in intensity, as well as starved.

He hitched up my skirt, baring my knees. I didn't care, lost in the veil of pleasure.

He devoured me, and I returned the caresses until a knocking at the door crashed through the maelstrom.

My chest heaved, and I gripped the wooden tabletop as he stared at me, the depths of his eyes promising that we were nowhere near done. He straightened his clothes, and I closed my eyes, vainly trying to recompose myself.

I didn't listen to the conversation between Raphael and whoever was on the other side, because easing the burn of my body was taking all my willpower.

The door closed once more, and I opened my eyes, but the man who'd been urging me to passionate heights had fled, replaced by a man encompassed by rage.

"Raphael?" I noted the tic at the corner of his jaw.

"My brother, Edward, has been busy." He held out a piece of paper. "He sent this."

I took the sheet, my hands still shaking as I read the missive aloud.

"Raphael, I know you have Francesca Whitmore there at the mansion. Her acts against Nobel Crest were unconscionable. She encouraged families to abandon our way of life, jeopardised the safety of the house. She stole our brother. Worst of all, she has compromised you..."

I raised my head. "This is some kind of joke, isn't it? I did none of these things." I fluttered the paper in the air.

"No, it's no joke. He believes it, even if it isn't the truth." He waved a hand. "Keep reading," he urged.

"Travis Haven has contacted me. He also seeks her, as her family did the same with Haven House. Restitution must be made. Release her to my judgement and be absolved." I rubbed my brow, which now ached. *"I will come for her in three days, unless you surrender her. Your brother, Edward Nobel."*

"We leave tomorrow morning, then. I need Damien's assistance, because while I can protect you from one or the other, my men are stretched already. We need a plan in place to nip this in the bud once and for all."

I sat there, useless and lost. I had nothing to add, no way to relieve Raphael of the burden.

"I'll give orders for the packing to begin." I nodded, numbed by the revelation of his brother's betrayal. "Francesca, we aren't done. Our wedding will be held soon. I'll discuss the details with Damien."

I stiffened. "I don't—"

Raphael bared his teeth in an approximation of a smile. "I told you. No going back."

Chapter Twelve

The dirigible rose, just as dawn crested. Raphael stood beside me, my hand firmly linked in his. "It's so beautiful," I whispered.

The land around us undulated, a thick layer of fog settling like a blanket over the earth while streaks of red and gold broke through the lightening indigo of the sky.

I shivered, and he tugged me against his side, arm sliding around my waist. Since yesterday, there'd been a clear and determined change in his attitude toward me, one I couldn't and had no wish to fight.

"When we're married, we'll come here regularly."

His words were drugging. Even though I'd railed against the restrictions of this far-flung place, it wasn't because of lack of beauty, acceptance, or even the people. Perhaps being here under different circumstances would be restful. "For short visits," I agreed.

"It's my home, Francesca. Has been since my birth, really. I want you to love it."

I heard the earnestness in his words and bit my lip. How could I explain without hurting him that such emotions came with time? "I have responsibilities in town, Raphael. People who need me."

He grunted. "You will also have a husband and family."

My gut contracted at that. Memories of the years in Haven, the nights the children and I had gone to bed hungry. The lack of heating in winter and the hand-me-downs. Raphael had insisted I wouldn't be entering a life like that, but it was all my brain could dredge up. Amaryllis, Damien, Andrew, and Gloriana had tried hard over the years to replace those memories with good ones, but the truth was it was a fearful existence many still lived. One I only remained a step away from.

"Come inside. You'll be chilled out here," Raphael urged, and I gave in, allowing him to usher me inside the beautifully appointed cabin.

Tea was served, a civilised affair with silver service and fine teacups. It wasn't the world I knew. Even Amaryllis and Damien, for all their money, rarely indulged in such highbrow rituals.

It didn't feel like me. It didn't fit in with the person I'd become, and that roiled in my brain. How on earth was I supposed to manage two polar opposites? Raphael, for all his rough-and-tumble exterior, was used to such niceties, having been raised in Nobel Crest. The mansion had reinforced that to me, whereas I, living by the graces of Ammy, couldn't possibly conceive of or feel comfortable in such rarefied atmosphere. It was... cloying.

Tea in hand, I sipped in silence, uncomfortably aware of Raphael's gaze on me when a knock came at the door.

"Enter," he called, and the man I knew as Jarvis entered, a scowl on his face.

"Sir, this just came on the Marconi. Cap'n thought you should see it immediately."

He held out the strip of paper, and Raphael placed his cup and saucer down with a rattle, then took the paper.

"God damn him," he muttered as he pushed up from his seat. He looked over at me. "Edward knows we're on the move. Someone from the mansion tipped him off, and he's demanding we detour immediately."

I gripped my cup harder. "But we won't, will we?" The audacity of Raphael's brother stole my breath.

"Certainly not, but it does mean we'll need to watch ourselves." He glanced at me, and I had the impression that he was trying to keep something from me, soothe my ruffled nerves in front of his man. "I'll be along in a moment to prepare a reply and send a further message," he growled to Jarvis, who touched his hat in my direction, then backed out of the room.

"What aren't you telling me?" I asked once Jarvis had gone.

Raphael sighed. "It's nothing I can put my finger on exactly, or be assured of. But this message means he's actively tracking us, and you. Haven is dangerous, but Edward is mean when roused. You only saw the tip that day. After you left, he raged for hours. I didn't realise it at the time, but there was more than just intent and grief behind his words."

I wanted to comfort Raphael, but what was there to say? I'd already worked out that his brother had taken a firm side against me. Nothing I said or did now would help the situation, so I kept my mouth closed, simply holding out my hand and taking his, hoping the action would convey my concern and support.

He squeezed my fingers, then let go and left me alone in the lounge, looking at my teacup and wondering where this would all end.

I drained the tea and rose, then headed for my chamber.

* * *

We landed just outside Haven, at the small private runway Damien had built on the edge of his property.

In the distance, the automaton dogs he used for security prowled, the light from their unnatural eyes shining in the gloom as I followed Raphael down the gangplank.

At the bottom, Damien and Amaryllis waited. In her arms, covered up, was the adorable bundle, Dawn. In the gig waited Constance, Faith, Simeon, and Sampson. They barely remembered the bad days before Mama died, and to them, life with Amaryllis and Damien was normal. On a good day, I could be thankful for that mercy. On a bad day, I wished I'd had the same experiences.

Damien swept me up into his arms. "Good to have you home, Frannie. Your mother and I have missed you."

I moved to Amaryllis, accepted the weight of Dawn in my arms and the fussing that was integral in Ammy. I felt comforted and safe in her arms, and she lavished attention on me.

"You've lost weight again, darling. We need to fatten you up. All those long hours in the clinic." Then she grinned at Raphael. "Raphael, dear, you look well. Keeping our girl safe, and for that, I have to thank you."

I couldn't contain my blush, and her knowing, keen eyes narrowed.

"Later," I interjected, and we hurried toward the horseless carriage, which Damien preferred. Sampson and Simeon called out from the gig while Constance and Faith climbed down, far more sober than I remembered in the past, but then I recalled their ages.

"Well, now, don't you two look lovely. New gowns?"

Constance nodded. "Oh yes, Ammy insisted we needed new wardrobes since Constance and I are starting art, music, and dance classes this coming winter."

"Indeed," I murmured. "But what about your academic lessons?"

"Ammy is bringing in new tutors for advanced lessons in geography, language, and history for me. Constance is going to take extra hours with the art tutor. Both Sampson and Simeon want lessons in engineering, so Papa is making enquiries."

"Well, then. That's excellent news."

Ammy ushered me into the carriage with Raphael, herself, and Damien. Dawn was passed back, but not before I noted the limp Ammy was carrying, as well as the looser fit of her gown.

I made a point to insist on checking her when we were settled at the house. The trip was quick, but the gig beat us. "They're still taking the shortcuts?"

Ammy frowned. "And racing at this hour of night. If I've spoken to them once, it's a million times," she growled.

"Boys will be boys, and the girls are growing out of their hoyden ways. I'm going to miss that." Damien chuckled.

Raphael stared at me, clearly surprised, but I kept my mouth closed. I would explain all later.

Once we reached the house, Ammy passed me Dawn, and I cradled her in my arms, aware of the interest Raphael was giving me, while Damien helped Ammy out of the carriage. Once I'd handed the sleeping babe down, I climbed out with Raphael at the rear.

We traipsed inside, and suddenly it was as if I'd never left. Noise echoed, and children called and yahooed while the staff bustled around, making me feel instantly at home again. The four of us, once Dawn was handed to the nurse, headed for Damien's office. The room, furnished with heavy wood and redolent with cigar smoke, was comfortable, and I took up my favourite spot on the chaise while Ammy and Damien settled in the armchairs. Raphael, with nowhere else to settle, lowered himself beside me.

Raphael's hand burrowed under the cover of my skirts and grabbed mine, holding me firmly in place, reminding me of the promise I'd given.

My mouth dried, because I knew what he was about to announce.

"Damien? Amaryllis? Before we talk about the situation at hand with Travis Haven and Edward, I would ask your permission to marry Francesca. I've already asked her, and she's agreed, but I want your permission as well." He moved slightly, uncomfortable with the declaration if the red cresting his cheeks was anything to go by.

Damien growled. "What have you done to her?"

Ammy shushed him and patted his hand. "Can't you see? He's fallen for our Frannie." There was glee in her words.

"But I hired him to protect her," Damien bit out.

"And I'm sure he'll be all the more protective of her since she's going to be his wife." She laughed at him, caressing his cheek. "Go on, give your permission, Damien, and admit it. Our little girl is all grown up."

That really embarrassed me, and I must have squeaked or made some utterance, as all eyes suddenly turned in my direction.

"You're not sure?" Damien enquired.

"Oh, it's not that. It's just... little girl?"

Ammy laughed, and Raphael sighed, his body relaxing beside me.

Damien watched for a long moment. "We'll discuss this later," he shot at Raphael, who nodded.

I was about to say something when Ammy stopped me with a pat on the lap. "Wedding preparations will be fun. Constance and Faith will attend you, of course. It'll be soon too, since you're both here."

It was like a juggernaut, with Ammy's excitement growing.

"We need to talk about the situation," Raphael interjected at the first opportunity.

"Who? What? How?" Damien was nothing if not direct.

"I believe Edward has made a pact with Travis Haven. He knew when we left the mansion to travel here, just the same as I believe he knew my destination to the mansion when we left town. If I don't miss my guess, they'll be actively looking for allies. They see you and Amaryllis as instigators of the plot. Andrew and Gloriana are probably also in the firing line."

Damien's mouth flattened. "Then it's a good thing I've been busy in the workshop with the boys. But what are your plans, given the circumstances?"

"They attacked the clinic," I added, and Damien's gaze settled on me.

"Did they?"

I nodded. "Miles was hurt, and Raphael has intelligence that indicates they'll attack the foundation, the house, and my staff if they don't get what they want. I've worked too hard to build up not just the reputation but also the network to simply walk away."

Damien's gaze swivelled to Raphael. "You have a plan?"

He shook his head, and the soft strands that escaped his queue brushed against my face.

"I have ideas, but nothing yet that could be considered a plan as such. But we do need assistance. More bodies. My men can't cover everyone at risk."

Damien smiled, baring his teeth. "Maybe not. But I can help you there."

Chapter Thirteen

"Why did you do that?" My question was out as soon as we exited the room, leaving Amaryllis and Damien within, chatting.

Raphael turned and pulled me into his arms. It was disconcerting, having others know we were together. The term "betrothed" felt just a step too far yet to acknowledge openly.

"I have no intentions of backing away. You promised, and I accepted." His gaze softened. "You're scared, and I understand that, Francesca. But we can overcome it. We just have to commit and explore where this leads."

It was the rumble of his words in his chest that banished some of the fears riding me. "Raphael..."

I didn't know what I was going to say, but he turned toward me, tipped my face up with a finger under my chin, and kissed me. It wasn't a cataclysmic and consuming kiss like we'd shared previously. Soft and tender, this caress melted the ice around my heart. I leaned into him, welcoming the touch, opening my mouth a little as he sipped at my lips.

When the kiss ended, I sighed.

"We'll marry soon, Francesca. I don't think I have the will to wait very long."

I almost laughed at his words, because a void I'd ignored had opened inside me. One I very much doubted anyone but he could fill.

I burrowed into his arms, wondering for the first time why he was the one to change me.

We retreated inside and regretfully parted at my chamber door. He was being accommodated further along in the wing, yet it felt too far apart.

The door closed behind me, and I divested myself of my gown, the large bath steaming in the middle of the room as promised. I sank into it, wondering if he was likewise engaged. My breath caught at that thought. *Does that make me fast?*

I wanted to protest, yet I wasn't one to hide from truths about myself. I acknowledged that I wanted every intimacy with him. But while I could embrace this truth, I had to temper it with the understanding that the danger he'd warned me of did truly exist.

I turned my mind to the situation at hand.

Travis Haven wanted to find me and make me pay for what he thought was Amaryllis and Damien's action against him. This wasn't any kind of normal behaviour. In my mind, it represented the sick logic of a twisted mind.

Then there was Edward Nobel. A man who despised me because he thought I'd taken advantage of his father at the end of his life. The thing was, it was his brother I—

Here I stopped myself before the thought could fully form. I wasn't yet ready to give word to the emotions growing inside me daily. We would marry soon, and I wondered if that might change Edward's mind, then dismissed that idea as fantastical. Clearly, for all Raphael had attempted to change his thinking, nothing had worked thus far.

Amaryllis was determined the wedding would be sooner rather than later, and once again, honesty forced me to admit I did too. I wanted no further impediments between Raphael and me. I could be fairly sure he felt the same, if the hardness of his body pressed against mine was an accurate gauge.

I rose from the tub, dried briskly, and began to dress when a knock echoed at the door. I tugged my wrapper over my undergarment-clad body and opened the door.

Raphael stood there.

The oxygen in my lungs escaped on a whoosh. "Raphael," I murmured. "I…"

His gaze roamed over me. "I apologise. I can return later."

I reached out and tugged him into the room. "You'll need to be quiet," I instructed and shut the door. "I need to finish dressing, and I'm guessing this is important from the look on your face."

His eyes flashed. "Indeed. But you were…" He saw the tub and glanced back at me. "You're dressing."

I reached the bed and scooped up the dress Fiona, Amaryllis's dresser, had left there for me. "I can change behind the screen," I told him. *Very fast indeed.*

The bed dipped beneath him as I ducked behind the large Chinese silk screen in the corner of the room and tugged off the wrapper. With a smile of devilry, I flung the cotton over the top of the screen. "So, tell me what's so important, Raphael."

I felt like a temptress, clad only in my cream-coloured undergarments with him seated within the same room. I pulled the gown up and thrust my arms into the tiny sleeves, adjusted the gown, then stepped out in the room. "I need your assistance. Will you button me?" I fluttered my lashes at him.

"You're playing a dangerous game, Francesca," he growled.

"Am I?" I answered coquettishly. This behaviour was alien, yet I felt driven to keep poking at him, urging a response.

He stepped up behind me, brushed my hair away, and began the process of slowly fastening each pearl bead into place. At the bottom, he stilled his hands before sliding them around my waist, parting his fingers.

If I'd considered myself short of breath before, it was nothing compared to the knowledge of the intimacy of his touch. I felt branded by the heat radiating.

He moved his hands upward, and I noted that we were before a full-length mirror. Our gazes met in the reflection, his hot and burning, mine soft and pliant.

Large hands slid over the silk of my dark blue gown, inching ever upward until they splayed just below my breasts.

"See me, Francesca. I'm not tame. I'm a man who wants the woman before him. I want to strip the gown from your body. I want miles of skin on display to touch. To claim." His dark, sensuous words lodged in my brain, driving rational thoughts out.

"I want you to do so, Raphael. I want to be with you."

His gaze deepened, the harsh planes of his face looking more like hard granite than ever before. If I'd been in any doubt of the physicality of our relationship, it fled. Or melted.

One hand skimmed over the mound of my breast, and the heat and want filled me. I closed my eyes, and my head rolled back against his shoulder. "Raphael... I want you."

The other hand moved down, fingers questing until my skirts were raised. "Open your eyes, my Francesca. See what I'm doing, how I'm touching you."

My body responded sluggishly, my gaze overlaid with a veil of hunger.

He'd managed to tug my skirt up and to the side so it bunched. I could see the legs of my drawers. His hand splayed over the bottom edge of my corset, and his fingers rubbed lightly at the hem of my underthings.

Tingling sensations started in my belly and seemed to radiate out. I gasped and would have closed my eyes once more, but Raphael demanded, "Keep them open, Francesca. Feel and see what I will share with you."

Behind me, even through the layers of garments, I could feel his own reaction, his body hardening as his breathing sped up, along with the beat of his heart.

"Raph..." My breath hitched.

"Yes. Between us, there will be no secrets, Francesca. I want you. Can you feel it?"

I jerked a nod. "Y-Yes."

"Soon we will be intimate, my flame. We will share our bodies and minds. Joined forever. Just us, Francesca. You'll be my only wife, as I will be your only husband."

A tear escaped. "How can you promise that?" My innermost fears were too close to the surface.

"Because this isn't just lust. I promise you, even if Edward died tomorrow and I took control, I will never take another to wife. Just you."

He kissed my cheek, my body on fire, then released me.

Without another word, he fastened the last of my buttons while I stood still, confused by the multitude of emotions his answer gave life to.

When he released me, I looked at him, but he smiled and moved back to the bed, settling himself. "Hair?"

I lifted shaking hands and sighed, then moved to the dressing table and fashioned a simple knot.

When I turned, he stood behind me, one hand in his pocket and an enigmatic smile on his face. "I have something for you."

He tugged his hand free of his coat and presented me with a ring. It wasn't ornate but rather fine with a small green stone in a filigree setting. "This was my grandmother's, left for me when I found the woman who'd become my wife. Wear it for me, please, Francesca?"

"It's beautiful," I breathed, and I meant it. Without another thought, I extended my hand, and he slid the ring onto my finger.

"And now everyone will know you're mine." There was a wealth of satisfaction in his words.

* * *

We settled at the table, the youngsters encouraged to join the adults on special occasions when the nursery was kept only for infants, such as Dawn.

Constance and Faith smiled and chose their seats at the end nearest Ammy , Simeon and Sampson took spaces on either side of Damien, while Raphael and I were seated opposite each other in the centre of the long table.

I felt terribly conscious of the ring on my hand, but no one appeared to notice it as the first course was carried out.

It was only as we finished that Constance squealed. "What's that?" she demanded, pointing to my hand.

My eyes found Raphael's, and I read on his face that he was happy for me to explain. "I'm betrothed to Raphael," I answered, blushing heavily and more than a little aware that the red of my face was unbecoming.

Cries of congratulations flowed until the main course arrived. "We'll have the wedding as soon as we can arrange it, so, Constance and Faith, you'll be excused from the schoolroom, as we'll need to organise gowns and arrange the service. Raphael, if you wish either of your brothers or friends to join us, make a list for me, and we'll see about getting them here in time. I'm thinking next Monday, which gives us eight days."

I jerked, because suddenly a date was chosen, and the planning would begin in earnest.

"I would appreciate Ellis being on hand to stand with me. Apart from that, my friends are few and difficult to reach." I wondered if that was because of the work he undertook in hunting down those breaking the laws but kept my counsel. Such information, Damien had explained to me aeons ago, was privileged, and most of the family was unaware of the extra "investigations" he and Amaryllis took on from time to time.

"Ellis is in Reginald's care. I'll send a Marconi to him in the morning, Raphael," I murmured. I was rewarded with a smile and glint in his eyes.

The conversation turned to day-to-day matters then. Constance and Faith had both chosen their fields of study and were eager to talk about their latest projects. Simeon and Sampson chattered about the girls hereabouts, and I saw, not for the first time, the truth in Constance's recent missive. The boys were growing into men while I was away. It hurt to recognise that I'd missed milestones in their lives.

I also kept an eye on Amaryllis. Her face was pale and strained, and Damien also kept an eye on her, I noted.

When the ices served as dessert were cleared away, I cleared my throat. "I'm somewhat fatigued tonight. Perhaps we might retire early, Damien?"

Amaryllis smiled. "I am too, and perhaps the girls and boys should head to bed . You too, Francesca. Perhaps, Damien, you might interest Raphael in a port. But I shall say goodnight." They all rose and left the room with barely a murmur. Raphael slanted a look at me that all but assured I wouldn't sleep any time soon, and Amaryllis linked her arm through mine.

She leaned on me during the walk to the stairs, but I held my tongue until we reached the top of the staircase. "Your leg hurts, Ammy. And you're pale. Come into my room for a moment so we can talk."

She didn't argue, and I frowned.

When she settled into the chair by the fire, I took the opposite. "Does the prosthetic not fit properly?"

She shook her head. "My leg aches because of the extra weight is all." I watched her surreptitiously rub at the limb.

"Let me see."

Amaryllis opened her mouth, then closed it, sighing as she reached for the hem of her gown. I dropped down and found the straps that had been used to hold the prosthetic lower limb in place, then removed it. The stump was a little red, and I sighed. "We need to replace the padding, Ammy. You know that. Now, I'll grab my tools and check the hydraulics."

I found my bag stashed in the bottom of the wardrobe and pulled it out. Rustling through, I found my tools. With quick and efficient movements, I checked the screws and prong wheels to ensure they were working optimally, making a mental note to use the data reader to check if there was more padding in the reposihouse. If not, I'd need to order several batches' worth, since Amaryllis tended to wait until it was essential to replace it in her limb.

I reattached the prosthetic. "I'm going to check what's on hand, and if there isn't any padding, I'll order it in. Perhaps we can have it sent with Ellis, Reginald, and Louisa?" I muttered to myself.

"You're sure about your decision, Frannie dear?" she enquired. It was just like her to be more concerned about my choices than her own health.

"Yes. I mean, I'm scared, and to be honest, I don't know if it's because of the whole Haven situation or because I'm changing the world I've grown comfortable in." It was more than I'd ever really disclosed, because, well, my life hadn't been either easy or simple before Ammy and Damien. Then after that, I'd tried to keep my distance because experience had taught me life was hard, and relying on yourself was the easiest way to survive.

"You know, if you have questions, you should ask me. Or Gloriana. We both love you and want nothing more than your happiness. Damien was going to check tonight with Raphael as to whether or not he plans to return to Nobel." I could hear her concern.

I blushed again, an occurrence that seemed to be making a regular appearance since meeting Raphael again.

"He's already assured me that is not what he plans," I told her, and she released a pent-up sigh.

"We were very concerned about that. I wouldn't want any girl, let alone you, to be subjected to that lifestyle," she confessed.

I patted her knee after I pulled her skirts back down. "No. Now, let's talk about how you're feeling."

She grinned. "Very well. Tired, but that appears to be normal at this point in gestation. Mornings are difficult but improving. And you're not here as my physician, dearest. You're here as our daughter."

I heard the words, and they warmed me again. Funny, I'd spent years keeping myself apart, working on the assumption that I was better off alone, yet here were people reinforcing connections I'd never really wanted before, and I felt... comforted.

"Thank you, Ammy." I slid my implements back in my case, gathering myself, then looked up. "You mean so much to me. I know it was hard when I was younger. I kept a distance, but I do appreciate everything you and Damien have done for me. Probably now more than ever before."

She sniffled and gave me a soggy smile. "Well, now, let's not get too soppy, shall we? After all, red eyes do nothing to encourage husbands." She rose. "I'll leave you now, but remember, above all, we do love you." She hugged me, quick and tight, and I returned it, aware that previously I would have tolerated it but tugged away as soon as I could. Not today.

"I love you, Ammy," I murmured, then let her go.

She smiled, another tear-laden action, then hurried from the room.

I dropped back into the seat by the fireplace and contemplated her words.

* * *

I'd almost dropped asleep when three quiet but intent knocks came at the door. I rose, bleary-eyed, and opened it. Raphael stepped inside and closed the door.

"You look sleepy," he said and gathered me close.

"I think I was drifting off when you knocked. What are you doing here at this hour?"

He grinned. "I needed to wish you a proper goodnight. I couldn't do that before."

"And if you're caught in here, there'll be hell to pay," I pointed out.

He laughed and kissed me.

I closed my eyes and leaned in closer. When we pulled apart, I whispered, "You could stay a little longer."

He caressed my face, and the impression of longing was followed swiftly by the one I now knew to be desire. "I won't. If I stay, I'll cross the boundary."

I wanted to argue, even opened my mouth, but he shushed me with a gentle finger on my lips. "No. Not tonight, my fire. Soon."

Frustration battered me, but the kiss he soothed me with also left me longing for more as he slipped out the door.

With careful moves, I stripped from my gown and let it slither to the floor. Once dressed in my night-rail, I climbed into the bed, but it was hours before sleep claimed me, and even in that, Raphael was the one I dreamed of.

Chapter Fourteen

A few days after the encounter in the bedroom, and as the wedding loomed, Raphael entered the morning room where I was settled with Constance, Faith, and Amaryllis. Gloriana was due soon, and scraps of material dotted every tabletop.

"Forgive me, ladies," he said with a dip of his head. "If I may talk with Francesca? It has to do with the clinic."

I rose once Amaryllis consented—not that it would have stopped me, but as she'd always pointed out, manners cost little—and followed him into the hallway. "What's wrong?" I asked, my voice low.

"There's been another attempt. This time, there's been damage. I'm waiting for details as to the extent."

My guts froze. "Who's hurt?"

He shook his head. "I believe we got lucky. My man on the ground said the clinic was empty. Ellis is ensconced in Damien's house, under guard, and is due to board the dirigible with Miles, Louisa, and Mrs Milesworth, for your foundation."

It was small comfort. "We need someone to secure all the drugs. Aloysius knows how to do that, if he can be sent in with a few other staff. My equipment as well, as replacing some of it will be difficult, most especially the items Damien gave me from his mother."

Raphael grabbed my hand. "I'll send that via the Marconi now. Is there anything else or anyone you need here for the wedding?"

I thought long and hard. "Aloysius, if he can be spared. There's also a small tote in my wardrobe. The few things from my mama are in it. I... There's a bangle and earbobs."

His thumb traced a circle on my hand. "I'll send for the bag and Aloysius, then." He smiled. "How is the planning?"

I rolled my eyes. "Anyone would think Amaryllis is planning a society event." Perhaps the words sounded pained, but there was little heat behind them. "Constance and Faith wanted me to have an elaborate trousseau, but I disabused them of that notion. As it is, I've agreed to no less than ten new gowns, though, and other items."

Raphael laughed. "The trials of a modern bride, I take it."

I snorted. "It could certainly be more tiresome. Amaryllis says a royal bride is likely to have at least forty day gowns and fifteen ball gowns." The thought still scandalized her.

He laughed. "I take it you're not planning on quite so many, then?"

"No, I think what's been ordered should be sufficient."

"Damien and I have been in discussions. We'll be leaving the morning after the ceremony. The *Lady Anthea* will be our suite for the evening of our wedding and under heavy guard. The following morning, my men will board, and we shall head for our next stop."

"Which is?"

His smile was pained. "Where we shall meet with the leaders of our team. But that's for later, not now, my fire. For now, focus on the wedding. On your friends' arrival and our future."

I smiled and cupped his cheek. "Always so optimistic."

He turned his head enough to kiss the palm of my hand. "As I should be when the most desirable woman in the world will become my wife in less than four days."

That sobered me. "I should return to Ammy and the girls. Gloriana is due shortly so we can finalise the seating plan for dinner and the menu."

"And Damien and I are checking the final security plans for the next few days. However, I shall return in time for lunch, and perhaps we might take a turn in the gardens."

His eyes twinkled, and I laughed. "I know that look, Raphael Nobel. But I have a dress fitting this afternoon, so it'll need to be closer to dinner."

"Then I shall await you at the appointed hour on the terrace."

He withdrew, and I watched for a moment longer, letting the sense of peace and goodwill fill me.

Then Gloriana swept into the hall. "Oh, Francesca. We should hurry and join the others, for there's much to do."

With that, we returned to the bustle of preparation.

Chapter Fifteen

I woke early and stayed lying in my bed. This was probably the last time I'd be able to call it that, as my eyes settled on the gown hanging on the dressing screen.

My bags had been packed, the last of the items I'd accumulated over the years collected together to travel to what would essentially be my new home base.

The tiny portrait of my mother, completed from a small photo discovered of her among the accoutrements of Haven House. A blanket she'd used to wrap each of us as babes. The last of my clothes. Books I had kept because they resonated with me or formed some part of my thought processes, and my journals. The writing set Ammy and Damien had gifted me when my first tutor had been engaged. It was all carefully packed into three large trunks for sending on to the mansion.

My entire life, I mused. It didn't seem much.

A knock at my door stirred me into action, and I was climbing from the bed as the door opened. In came Ammy, Faith, and Constance, followed closely by Ammy's dresser, Fiona, and three of the maids bearing chairs and folding tables.

"On this auspicious morning, we thought to surprise you with breakfast before we begin the preparations," Ammy announced grandly.

She might be early in her third decade, but she took the role of matron very seriously.

We settled down, my wrapper covering my gown, and a table unfolded before me. Silver trays held plates of pastries and more filling choices of eggs and bacon. Carafes of coffee and tea were dispensed, and much gaiety ensued.

Finally, the girls rose, and Fiona along with another maid tugged the dressing screen into the middle of the room. The hip bath was carried in and the detritus from breakfast cleared away.

Ammy chatted inconsequentially as I bathed behind the screen.

"You will, of course, need to send thank-you notes for all the gifts once you return from your trip, Francesca."

"Yes Ammy. And I will ensure Raphael organises the notice for the papers. Unless he's already attended to that."

Though it seemed odd to have someone with me at this time, I also welcomed it, as nerves quivered within me.

When I'd finished, Fiona wrapped me in a fine towel while once more moving the screen. After I dried, a chair was placed beside the screen, and the finest undergarments awaited me, every piece exquisitely embroidered and light. Once I'd donned the first layer, Ammy rang the bell, and the girls were summoned to the room, the bath was removed, and the gaiety resumed once more.

"Frannie, where are you going?" Constance enquired.

"Will you remember to take images with the kinetoscope camera?" Faith called.

"I don't know, Constance. Yes, I will attempt to remember, Faith."

Fiona settled me in the chair before the vanity, the brush in her hand. Her movements were sure and light, and it made me think of Leona. Raphael had offered to send for her, but we'd finally agreed once the danger had passed that it might be the best time to set her up permanently in our household as my dresser.

Privately, I doubted I'd need one, but Raphael had insisted that my new status might require such assistance. I simply shrugged that off for now.

In the meantime, she'd been informed to take stock of my gowns, arrange any repairs that may be needed, and to oversee the setting up of my rooms.

"Miss Francesca, do keep your head still," Fiona muttered with a little touch of frustration, bringing me back to reality. Unused to such attention, I felt uncomfortable and hoped it would pass soon. Or at least this current torture, given I was used to dressing my own hair daily.

With my hair prepared, I turned and received the approbation of Ammy and my sisters, then settled myself in a chair while their hair was styled, their gowns donned. Then it was my turn.

My ensemble was a heavy cream silk in two pieces—a bodice and skirt—tightly cinched at the waist and decorated with pearls and crystals, with ruffles at my feet. As I was being laced, the girls "Oohed" and "Aahhed" over the style.

"I read that in Paris, such gowns are the height of fashion. Ammy even used the datascreen to show the modiste."

I did roll my eyes at that, for I'd been there at the time. But keeping quiet and not upsetting my sisters was important to me.

My shoes were things of beauty. With a carved heel and the same silk covering as my gown, they were the perfect accompaniment. And in my hair, I wore a simple garland of orange blossom, which had been sent direct from the mansion for today.

Ammy stared at me. "Such a beautiful bride. Damien and I are so proud of you, dearest Francesca. You entered our lives with such a strong will and a determination to be the person you've become. One who cares deeply. We have a gift for you." She retrieved a small box I'd overlooked from the table and handed it to me.

I opened it. Inside lay a beautiful locket, the filigree finely etched and made to match the bangle I'd kept from my mother. It was so thoughtful that tears of happiness and gratitude burned my eyes. "Ammy, it's so beautiful."

"Perfect, then, for a beautiful bride." She lifted it from the box and limped behind me, opening the clasp and settling it around my neck. "This comes with all our love, my dear. Never question that wherever you are and whatever you do, we will always be there to support and love you both."

She rested her hand on my shoulder.

Fiona came forward with the bangle, which I slid onto my wrist. Then I slipped the earrings into place.

"Come, let's see the final result," Ammy urged, and I turned to the mirror and gasped. Before me stood the image of me, only different. Softer and ready for the next phase of my life.

Constance opened the door after a knock, listened to whoever hovered outside then withdrew. "The guests are all here and seated, Ammy. We should head downstairs."

I inhaled deeply. This was the moment of no return. *Do I want to say no?* This was my last chance, but instinctively I knew I had no intention of walking away. Raphael waited for me, and as for what our future would bring, well, there was no way I could be totally sure, but he'd made promises to me, just as I had already to him.

I took the sheaf of flowers, the carefully crafted bouquet, and brought it to my face. Inhaling deeply, I sighed. "It's time," I whispered and followed the other women from the room.

From that point on, I might as well have been living in a dream. Down the staircase we moved, slower than normal, allowing for Ammy's infirmity. Once on the flagged floors, we noted Damien waiting for us, dashing in his black suit with tie.

"My beautiful girls. Nanny is waiting outside with Dawn, my love," he said to Ammy, then turned to Constance and Faith. "You both look very fetching in your gowns." They did, their pale pink bustled gowns accenting their attractive figures, a perfect foil for their milky skin.

Damien took my arm and patted my hand into place. "You are a truly beautiful bride, Francesca. One I am proud to call my daughter."

Tears burned again, and I had to blink several times to will them away.

"Thank you, Father," I whispered, and this time, he choked up.

We took up positions as the musicians began to play just outside the front door.

Slow, steady steps took us out into the sunlight. And waiting for me at the end of the short aisle was Raphael.

* * *

Walking back to the dirigible with the man I now called husband was like drifting through some dream. The sounds of those behind us were muted, and ahead, the craft looked large and imposing.

I wanted to stop, to just take a moment, yet it felt like my life was speeding toward some conclusion—an ending as much as a beginning. The weight on my chest grew. Not from fright but the acceptance that the life I'd lived before was almost over.

Now that I was Dr Francesca Nobel, it seemed I was once again stepping further away from my history and toward a gaping chasm, where depths and obstacles were hidden from view.

If I'd learned one thing about myself, it was that life wasn't simple or straightforward. What the future held was uncertain.

We reached the gangplank, tents scattered around the craft.

"The men?" I enquired.

"Tonight, they will guard the craft."

In his voice, I detected a hesitancy I'd never before heard. It soothed the ragged edges of my own thoughts, because if he too was affected by the gravity of the moment, then I wasn't alone in all this.

We made our way up the steps and into the empty craft. He led me to the dining room, where a luscious spread waited, along with a bottle of champagne chilling in a deep bucket of ice and two finely etched glasses.

A meal of cold foods also sat on the table. I took everything in, an image etched in my mind. The stark white of the linen. The blush pink roses in a silver and crystal vase.

Scents filled the air, and I turned, noting that the roses on the table were just the beginning. Arrangements sat on every available surface. Candlelight flickered, the gas lights having not been lit.

Raphael—my husband—moved to a cabinet and opened it. Inside sat a large item I knew to be a phonograph. He touched a button, and I watched, mesmerised. "It's not run with a crank handle?"

He turned and laughed. "No. This one has been specially crafted to run on a discharge engine, using the flow of current stored in the capacitor to direct the energy to the terminals."

Strands of music filled the air. The waltz was one I knew well.

When Raphael took me in his arms and we began to move, I was struck by the sensuality of the dance. The way our bodies flowed together, each mirroring the other. By the end of it, I was breathless, not from the physicality of the moves but the sheer eroticism.

His eyes glowed as he stepped back. Then he turned, poured two glasses of champagne, and handed one to me. My hand shook a little as his fingers brushed against mine.

"You look beautiful today, my fire." I closed my eyes. The intimacy of his words, the way his breath slid over my skin, torched every nerve ending.

"Thank you," I murmured. "You looked quite dashing." He had. The fit of his clothing had stolen my breath as I'd made my way toward him. The black suit had flowed over his musculature in a way that I was sure made other women in the congregation come near to a faint. My lips curled upward at that thought.

"What's going on in that talented brain of yours, wife?"

His gentle reminder of my new status startled me, and I jerked, spilling a little liquid on my hand. "Oh," I said. "I was thinking about today."

"And?" His smile was wolfish, and I wondered if he knew what I was thinking. I blushed, and he laughed faintly. "About me?"

I gulped and nodded. "Your suit is... well fitted."

He quirked a brow. "You like that?"

"I do." I took a sip of the wine. It was tart on my tongue but refreshing. "You're exceptionally handsome."

"Perhaps, but you're exquisite. The sheen of your hair, the fineness of your features. The perfection of your body. The keenness of your mind. They all are a part of what draws me to you, Francesca."

"Oh." His words filled me with warmth. "I'm not really hungry," I stated. "Perhaps I might go bathe?"

I needed time. Not alone as in he should leave, just a space to clear my mind, to prepare for what was ahead. Besides, I wasn't prevaricating when I said I wasn't hungry. The luncheon Ammy provided had been more than ample.

"Of course." Raphael took my glass and placed both of ours on the table. Then he slid my fingers into the crook of his arm, and together we headed to the chambers.

I expected him to leave me at the gold cabin, but he shook his head when I started to pull away. "Our room."

My stomach lurched before memory of our marriage surged forward. Once more I became aware of the weight of his ring on my hand and all it symbolised. Unity. Forever. The words we'd spoken to each other before those gathered to share our joining.

The door opened, and as in the dining room, the scent of flowers filled my senses along with more flickering firelight.

My trunk was sitting at the end of the bed, a tangible reminder of what was yet to come. My nerves jumped and quivered.

"I had your clothes hung in the wardrobe and your dressing screen placed in the corner." Hanging from my screen was my nightrobe and wrapper. I cleared my throat and turned to him.

"I have something left to finalise but will return soon." I knew he was giving me time and privacy, and for that I was more than a little thankful. After all, this was our first night as husband and wife. The intimacies of the marriage bed lay before me, and while I knew the technicalities of it, I'd never before partaken.

With trembling fingers, I settled about releasing the buttons of my bodice, then laid it on the trunk, followed by the skirt.

I turned my attention to my undergarments and blushed again at the way Ammy had insisted on the fragile fabric with a knowing smile.

In the bathroom, I drew a deep bath, dropped scented salts into the water, and settled deep, sighing and resting my head on the cushioned edge.

My thoughts swirled. Was I ready?

A sound drew my attention, and before I could say anything, Raphael entered the bathing room.

I sat up, using my hands to cover my breasts and crotch.

He carried my glass of wine, and my eyes widened, taking in his state of undress. His legs showed below the hem of his robe, which was tied with a silk ribbon at his waist, the hint of his chest bared for my gaze.

"Raph... Raphael. What are you...?"

"I brought your wine, my fire."

He reached out, and I took it from him, then realised I'd revealed my chest to his fiery gaze.

"Don't," he instructed. "Don't hide such perfection from me." The words were a murmur as he looked his fill.

My body burned where he glanced, and I felt something unfamiliar but emboldening. He liked what he saw.

I handed my glass back, and he placed it on the vanity unit. I took his hand and levered up, allowing my breasts to slide from the water, baring them further, so my nipples puckered with the touch of air.

"Beautiful," he growled and lowered himself beside the tub. He reached for my flesh, grazing it lightly.

I gasped as lightning zinged beneath the layer of skin. "Raphael?"

"I want to adore you, Francesca. To know the secrets hidden and to give you joy. Completion."

His mouth touched mine, and my eyelids drooped shut. I couldn't control my body's intense reaction to the erotic assault on my senses.

His lips played over mine, taking his time, sipping at me before his tongue surged deep. My hands came up, twining around his neck, and his continued their seductive exploration of my body, tracing down toward my belly and splaying across.

He tugged away. "Here. This is where we begin, my fire."

As Raphael moved back, I mewled at the loss of contact. He divested himself of his gown, letting it pool at his feet, and for the first time, I saw the magnificence of the man. His body was firm and hewn yet covered in silken flesh. His maleness, hard and jutting forward, told me of his desire. His eyes were slumberous. He reached for me, and without needing him to ask, I rose, rivulets of liquid sluicing down my body. When he gently enfolded me in a towel, it was close to rubbing electricity into my skin, so highly sensitised as it was.

He hefted me in his arms and carried me to the bedroom before sliding me down his body. There I stood, mute but a willing partner in our foreplay.

The towel dropped to the floor, and I reached out, touched the flesh of one hard pectoral muscle, then splayed my hands across his chest, feeling the rapid heartbeat below. I looked up, and our gazes meshed. "Raphael?"

"Only for you, my fire," he responded, and I felt the way his body tensed as I moved my hand down toward his abdomen.

"Perfect," I muttered. "Every muscle defined." I bit my lip as his erection jerked beneath my careful ministrations. "In peak condition." I smiled. "You must work hard to stay like this." I barely recognised my voice, husky with desire while my body demanded more than I was giving. My nipples were hard points of pleasure. "I should investigate," I mused and moved in, crowding into his space and letting my flesh glance against his, those hard points grazing him. I jerked back, and he hissed.

The tingles and invisible wires inside me tugged and demanded more.

"Francesca." The rumble of his voice captured my attention. "Come." He crooked a finger, and I followed, highly aware of our mutual nudity, caught in the magic of his body, the movement of his buttocks as he led the way to the side of the bed.

He sat on the side, and I settled beside him, nerves aquiver as he pulled me close, his mouth against mine. "Relax," he whispered, the touch softer than a butterfly wing.

He cupped my shoulder but didn't push me for more, as if he read my confused response. I wanted this connection but also feared the pain I'd heard of.

The movement of his fingers broke through my thoughts again, and I let myself sink into the moment. To simply enjoy the touch and be.

"Francesca, I want you." His lips moved now, trailed across my cheek and found the line of my jaw, then the sensitive spot just by my ear. When he touched there, I arched, and his hand cupped my breast. For the first time, his thumb settled on a peaked nipple.

I gasped, "Oh, Raphael. I feel..." But words failed me as I melted inside. My legs parted, and I felt an emptiness deep inside my belly.

"Feel my hand touching you, Francesca. Loving you."

"Oh... oh God... yes," I stammered.

I didn't know when or how I moved, but now I lay on the counterpane, and he was looming over me. I reached out and placed my hand on his shoulder, revelling in the heat and power there, how the sinews extended and trembled.

One of his hands slid down my side, cupped my hip, then continued its exploration down my thigh before making its way back up until it glanced across virgin flesh. I hissed and writhed, my body reacting instinctively now.

The fire inside me grew, threatening to engulf me. "I..."

"Shhhh," Raphael growled against my skin. Then his tongue found a peak and flicked at the nub as his hand rubbed the spot between my legs. At that moment, I dug my nails into his shoulders, and Raphael crooned, "Let go, my fire."

Had my body simply needed that encouragement? My mind fractured, senses exploding as I convulsed beneath his ministrations.

I couldn't tell how long I hung there, but when I returned to myself, I breathed heavily, and an unusual languor spread through my body. Every muscle relaxed, and the tension within my belly melted away. For a moment, I remained still, eyes shut tight. When I opened them, he watched me, face darkened with the flush of hunger, jaw tight, but his eyes shone. There was an inner knowledge that this was my first time, and he'd brought me this flash of extreme pleasure.

"Was that...?" I asked shyly.

"Not nearly, my fire. This time, we'll fly together." His expression turned rapacious, and his mouth forced mine apart.

I welcomed him this time, as my body responded in kind. I grabbed him closer while a finger played a game of exploration at my most intimate flesh, touching and probing while I arched and writhed.

"You're so wet," he crooned, and I felt the subtle shift of his body.

My legs widened, making room for him as my hands began to roam, sliding down the flesh of his back, feeling the bunching of muscles beneath my questing fingers. His buttocks were round and firm, and I cupped them as he moved in time with some unknown melody.

When the head of his cock nudged against my body, I felt no fear.

"I'm going to enter you, my fire. It'll hurt, but that will pass. Trust me."

I did. I wanted him and the pleasure I'd already encountered.

He flexed his hips, and I felt the nudge as my body tried to deny entrance. The sensation of him, the girth, stretched me, and it already burned, yet he'd barely begun to breach my maidenhood.

"Francesca, feel me," he demanded, pushing slowly but surely while my body ached.

I squeezed my eyes shut. "It… it hurts, Raphael."

He grunted. "Trust me. One push." Then he moved, surged deep, swallowing my cry with his mouth.

Tears leaked unabated. My entire body had tensed, and now the pleasure was gone. I shoved against him, but he stayed firm. Still.

For long moments, I wanted no more, but soon the pain receded. The involuntary tightening of my body released, and I breathed.

"I'm going to move," he whispered, and I braced myself for more pain, more sting.

It didn't come. Instead, there was a friction, sensuous and drugging.

I held still. "It'll hurt again soon," I whispered.

"No. The pain is done. Gone. Now there is only pleasure." A flex of his hips, the slide of his body stole my breath while pleasure mounted again.

He moved, holding me, teaching me. Every kiss was calculated to increase my arousal, and this time, when the explosion happened, I gave in and welcomed it.

Raphael continued his frenzied movements while a scent, new and exotic, filled the air. The musk of a man in the throes of passion. When he came, he cradled me close, and the sensation of his orgasm set off tiny reactions within my body. Then he collapsed, holding me tight.

* * *

I woke to the unfamiliar sensation of a finger running through my hair. I turned, and there he was. Raphael. My husband.

"Hello," he whispered.

I blushed. "Hello."

"You're amazing. Truly."

I laughed at that. "No one has ever called me that. I mean…"

He grinned. "No. Not like this. Francesca, you are my fire." The mirth died away, replaced by a look I couldn't quite name but felt a whole lot like being cared for. "What we have? This pleasure? It's just the start. We have a lifetime to explore."

Tears filled my eyes.

"You're crying. Did I hurt you?" His face paled.

"No. It's... I don't know how to explain, Raphael. Yes, there was pleasure of the kind I'd no notion of. But it's more than that." I struggled to find a way to sum up what was growing inside me, this emotional well that grew bigger the more it filled.

He nodded. "I feel that too."

I slid gentle fingers over his brow, knotted at the gravity of the conversation.

"I have these feelings for you, Francesca. They urge me to protect you. To hold you close. To be with you."

I blinked slowly, because I also felt things I was too scared to name. Deep feelings that demanded I give as much as I took. I'd never been like the other girls, cooing over the men who danced attendance on them. I'd given all my time to study, then honing my skills. But with Raphael, there was a tempering of my driven nature.

I refused to speak what hovered at the corners of my mind, though, unwilling to cheapen the moment or our relationship until I was certain I could give him what he deserved.

Instead, I snuggled down. "Thank you."

He laughed. "Oh no, my fire. Let me thank you. Now we should sleep. We'll have an early morning, and neither of us is ready to be taken unaware."

Sleep didn't come easily or quickly, though, caught up in his arms. I listened to the steady beat of his heart, where his body pillowed me. Finally his breathing changed, became softer, and I knew he slumbered.

The shock of our naked bodies entwined felt scandalous, but I needed this time to weed through what had occurred.

We'd connected as only two adults could do. But how deep did the connection go? That was yet another question I couldn't answer.

I lay there, my mind slowing and my body fatigued, until I finally dropped into a dreamless sleep.

Chapter Sixteen

I didn't know why, but breakfast seemed oddly intimate. We'd been as close as any two people could get, and memories of the touches and kisses made me tingle, yet eating a pastry and drinking tea at the same table carried an emotional importance I wouldn't have expected.

"So, where are we headed to?" I asked.

Raphael sighed. "We'll travel to New York. I need to see the head of our team."

I waited, sure he'd tell me more.

But he didn't, the silence stretching out between us.

"So?" I prompted, and he smiled, as if he'd won some kind of internal wager with himself.

"Marcus Bloom is the third son of the scion of Bloom Ridge. Some time back, before Ammy and Damien, he became aware of a secret order that most of the heads of the cults belong to. These cults may be closed to the wider world, but in some form or other, they need to abide by the laws—or at least enough to ensure their 'God-given rights' aren't infringed upon by the government."

Surprise filled me. "Wait, like some kind of association or union?"

His nod was joined by a frown. "My father was a member, but only long enough to learn what he could. He didn't believe in the cults, as

I've told you. He wanted to disband that side of Nobel Crest and release the women, give them options and opportunities. The SELED group—"

"What?"

"SELED. Sect Leader Designates."

"Holy hell," I whispered. "You said... I know they have a group or union, but that's just... dreadful!"

He nodded. "It is. My father left SELED and gave information to Bloom. Edward made representations immediately after Father's death, and Nobel Crest was readmitted within weeks. He, like many of us, came from money. It's money that begets money, so he's got the resources. We aren't just second and third sons, though. We're parents, partners, and concerned citizens. But few are in the position Damien and I are. Were."

I arched a brow. "Were?"

"When we marry, we can no longer be called upon as agents. We become strategists or supporters."

"But Edward...?"

"Yes." Raphael nodded. "We must get the information to Marcus. Anything less isn't an option."

"But how will they sort out the mess at Nobel Crest if you're no longer able—"

"I plan to request Marcus's assistance, similar to what he did with Damien, given the circumstances, the immediate danger to many. That's where you come in. You'll need to give testimony to the injuries and damage—"

"I can't. The doctor-patient confidentiality rules—"

Raphael raked a hand over his face. "We could subpoena the information, if that's what you need."

I sat up in my chair. "Why? Why would you do that to me?"

He grimaced. "We need to put together an argument. Show his pattern of behaviour has changed. You offer one side."

"Don't ask this of me, Raphael," I pleaded.

"But how else do I...?"

I sighed and looked down at my tea. "I will contact Ellis. If he grants me an agreement that I can divulge some of his information, I will. He then tells what he knows. If I go sharing these women's cases, no one will trust me. My practice will be destroyed, and the clinic, not to mention the foundation, won't be worth anything. No one will support it. No one will use it."

He stared at me. "Surely not," he uttered, seemingly astonished.

"Yes. I know of a doctor who divulged a small piece of information about his patient without cause. He was struck off." I clapped my hands together. "Just like that."

"Then I'll contact Ellis—"

"No. I will need to. I'll send word to my father through the Marconi and request that he ask Ellis to respond. That will free me up to give the information required. Then you'll ask Ellis about the women, and that should solve the problem, right?"

"I hope so," Raphael muttered.

After breakfast, Raphael and I made our way to the bridge. This time, I met the captain. He was gruff and rough but offered to allow me to use the Marconi once I explained my difficulties and that I was trained in its use.

Ellis, need permission to share details of your injury. Putting together a case for Raphael concerning Nobel Crest. Require answer urgently.

The Marconi wasn't the best way to transmit something like this, and to be honest, it could so easily be intercepted. But we hadn't travelled too far, so I sent the message and hoped for a positive outcome.

We'd just settled in the lounge, me with a book I'd requested Louisa locate for me on the musculature injuries to feet, when a runner knocked on the door and entered. "Miss... er, Mrs... Dr—"

I took pity on the flustered young man. "Yes. You have something for me?"

He nodded and thrust the tape into my hands.

Permission granted. Tell Raphael I have much information.

I looked up and saw Raphael watching me. His gaze narrowed.

"Ellis?"

I handed the tape over, and he frowned. "It's welcome news but also worrying. How many more secrets has my brother hidden?"

Once we were again alone, I rose, stepped over to him, and cupped his cheek. "We'll deal with this together, Raphael."

* * *

Our arrival in New York wasn't quite what I expected. The buildings and hustle were just as busy as I'd thought, but it was the carriages of men in dark suits, the variety of weapons, and one particularly nasty-looking man who ushered us toward the vehicle in the centre that took me by surprise.

"Loren Filobus," he said gruffly. "I'm to be your escort during your time in New York. I've stationed ten men with a variety of weapons, including the harquebus, on your dirigible."

"My wife, Dr Francesca Nobel," Raphael introduced.

"Dr Nobel, I hear you've helped to assist those who've been damaged by the evolving rules of Nobel Crest."

I gazed at him steadily. "I'm not at liberty to discuss such things with you. My patient has only given me permission to discuss these issues with Marcus Bloom."

Raphael's subtle smirk told me my answer was not just expected but preferred.

"Of course, Doctor. We've been in contact with your brother, Mr Nobel. Ellis has agreed to share intelligence with Marcus. He's sent a group of rangers down to protect him and to assist your men with the Whitmore Foundation and Clinic. I believe Damien has the house under protection?"

Raphael nodded. "He's equipping the house with his new generation of automaton canines."

Loren quirked his brow. "Indeed? I saw the first generation in action. They proved quite effective."

Raphael smiled. "He's also added a wireless power transmitter to the fencing."

"Now that I'd truly like to see," Loren answered.

The streets were busy, and I sat forward in my seat, hoping to glimpse the tall buildings, as I'd never been to New York before.

"If you wouldn't mind, Doctor, would you please sit back?" Loren said. "We aren't planning on advertising your presence here if we can avoid it."

I glanced at Raphael, who nodded, and I regretfully pushed back into the squabs. We rounded a corner, and a large black metal fence came into view. The carriage swung within, and I watched as two of their procession took up positions at the exterior.

The carriage rounded a corner in the driveway and came to a stop under a white portico. The door opened, and Loren Filobus, followed by Raphael, climbed down. Then I followed suit.

Nerves now rattling, I was thankful that Raphael took my hand, and together we entered a large, imposing building finer than the house Ammy and Damien lived in, and not dissimilar to Raphael's own home.

Ushered into a room, I noted a chair facing the opposite direction, but when it swung around, I was surprised to see a middle-aged man with thinning grey hair and his hands steepled.

"Well, Raphael. You surprised me. This must be your wife, Dr...?"

"Dr Nobel," I answered.

He smiled. "Indeed. I'm Marcus Bloom. Felicitations on your recent marriage. I trust your journey was event-free?"

"Very much so," I answered, my hand held in a tight grip by Raphael.

"I believe you have something to share with me relating to your husband's brother Ellis? I knew their father well, Edward not all, and Ellis is still too young to enter the circles I inhabit."

I wondered at what that might mean, then shook myself. Now wasn't the time to deal with the semantics of his answers. "Ellis came to me suffering deep pain. He'd been injured, yet his and Raphael's brother refused him treatment." I felt awful saying this. I knew Raphael was more than a little aware of the man Edward had become, but it seemed so wrong to be denigrating him in front of his brother.

"How did it happen?"

I tugged my hand free of Raphael's and twisted the handkerchief in my hands. This is the part I hadn't even shared with my husband. "He was meeting a girl. One he liked a lot, but Edward didn't feel she was suitable for Ellis. He sent Ellis out to complete a task. During that task, the equipment Ellis was using failed. He suffered deep and grievous injuries that could have been easily dealt with. Edward, however, refused to honour his father's request that I should be called to assist should there be any medical issue. He was aware of my plans to become a physiotraducere, and Adam financially assisted me to achieve that end. Adam and I were close before he died. He was like a father or grandfather to me, and it was the only thing he ever asked of me."

Marcus stared at me. "So, Edward believes what exactly? That you'd been chosen for him?"

Before I could respond, Raphael snarled. "Not at all. My father believed in Francesca. Saw what most others didn't, the spark and inspiration. Father simply wanted her to succeed and understood that a crucial factor of that was to place her in charge of the medical situation once she'd qualified."

I swung around to stare at Raphael. "What?"

"He knew you. There were letters left for me, received only once he'd passed and another batch with Damien for me after you qualified. He knew the resentment you'd face from Edward and me." His cheeks pinked.

"Oh." There wasn't much else to say.

"So, Edward refused to contact you?" Marcus prompted.

"That is correct. He threatened those in town on my arrival not to seek my assistance," I explained.

"Then Ellis arrived?"

"Raphael received a message, and I travelled with him to offer medical care to his brother. When I arrived, it was clear the wound was serious. Infection had set in." I shrugged. "To have survived as long as he did, in that condition, is only thanks to the ladies who tend minor injuries."

"And while you were there, other cases came to light. Women who'd been damaged?"

"I cannot discuss them with you. My doctor-patient oath prevents that." I bit my lip and looked down at my hands, clenched around the small lacy handkerchief.

"What my wife cannot tell you was relayed to me. Ellis saw them during his early convalescence. Women who'd been beaten into submission. Some pregnant. At least some of them were forced, we know. Ellis has been conferring with them. They're all willing to give testimony." His words shocked me to the core. I hadn't thought they would agree, so I hadn't enquired. "The only thing Ellis asks is that young Michaela and her family are removed beforehand. Edward doesn't exhibit rational thought, and Ellis is concerned that he'll take retribution on them. Michaela's father is a farmer, neither well educated nor well placed to protect his daughter."

My heart sank. Ellis was honest and far too young to be in this position. He wouldn't know how to protect the young woman, except offer her the protection of his name. Something I was sure he wasn't really ready for. But like his brother, chivalry would come at a high price.

"I've already made arrangements for her. I have three of my best currently travelling. Jarvis will facilitate it and ensure she's outside the gates when they arrive. So will her family. I'll have her removed, and they'll move the family into the hotel until we know she's safely away."

Tears pricked my eyes at Raphael's assertion. I could only hope it would succeed—or his men, at any rate. I turned to him. "When will you send them?"

"They arrived this morning, Francesca. She should be in hand by now."

I nodded and waited.

"So, the women will give evidence? Are there physical signs?" Marcus folded his hands on the desk.

I cleared my throat. "Giving no specifics, yes, there were. If they agree to allow me to give a medical opinion, then I'd be willing to give the descriptions of injuries."

"Then, together with Ellis's testimony, we can make representations that the actions are contrary to their charter. They can't afford to lose their recognition under law as religious entities, and should this be released publicly, the outcry would damage their standing with lawmakers."

My stomach turned at Marcus's dry summary, yet I knew this was the way with legislated bodies such as the little-known SELED.

"So, you have some kind of power with the elected officials?" I lurched forward in my seat.

"My dear, sometimes there are bodies created outside of government purely to keep those in power honest. My role is to ensure that SELED acts according to their charter. If they don't, and the news reaches me, I have ears in Washington. Very influential ears."

"Marcus, he's going after my wife, along with Travis Haven."

Now Marcus's eyes gleamed. "Junior?"

Raphael gave a disgusted snort. "The other bastard is dead."

Marcus reclined in his chair, clearly thinking. "You think you can take them—both of them—alive?"

Raphael hissed. "If I don't, and terminal force is required, there will be a damn good reason." Steel edged his words, and I turned to him. He took my hand. "My wife will be safe. As will her foundation and clinic. He'll have to get through me to reach her."

Breathing was an impossibility, because in my mind, that was exactly what I saw. Raphael shot or hacked, bleeding out, and me unable to stem the flow.

My leg started bouncing up and down, frustration and fear warring for equal footing.

"I'll need to gain agreement from the other benefactors," Marcus said. "I'll send word later today."

Clearly we'd been dismissed, so I rose along with Raphael, who kept my hand firmly in his.

Before we left the room, Marcus cleared his throat. "She's a firecracker, boy. Will keep you on your toes, but a powerful ally, I think."

I opened my mouth, but Raphael tugged me through the door and into the hall.

Loren had perched himself on the seat opposite and stood when he spied us. "All done, then?"

"Yes. My wife and I wish to—"

Loren shut him down before he could ask for whatever he'd had in mind. "Now isn't the time, sir. I'm to escort you back to your dirigible, wait while your people conduct an inspection and safety check, and then see you safely on your way."

Raphael's lips thinned. "Very well, if that's the way it's to be."

Chapter Seventeen

We were several hours out of New York, sitting on the small deck and taking in the air close against the sides, when a bang echoed all around. The ship lurched, and I fell from my seat and rolled toward the railings. It was a wild roll, and for long seconds, I feared it was to my death.

"Francesca!" Raphael's bellow echoed in my ears as I hurtled toward the uprights and grabbed a hold, hand sliding around the polished wood in a death grip. I had no intention of falling to the ground so far below.

Terror had my body shaking as adrenaline raced through my system.

When Raphael grabbed me and dragged me back against the side of the quarters, I trembled, and it took long moments before I warmed again and the quiver ceased while he held me close, his chin resting on my head. "Oh my God, Francesca. I... I was terrified you'd fall."

The ship shuddered and shook, like a creature in its death throes, and I clutched Raphael's arm. "What's happening?"

"I don't know yet, but come on and we'll find out."

He anchored me against his side, as if that alone would ensure my survival. Though he had so far.

In the distance, there was clear ground. I just hoped if we had to make an emergency landing, that was the location!

Smoke filled the interior of the cabins, and I choked, my grip on Raphael tenuous as sweat made my hands clammy.

He dragged me forward, always ensuring my body was caged safely within his embrace as we climbed the ladder to the bridge.

"Captain? What the hell is happening?" His demand broke through the air.

The captain turned. "Sir, we need to make a landing. Something or someone has rendered the engine inoperable."

The craft canted again to the side, and my footing slipped, but Raphael kept me close with one arm while holding on to a security bar with the other.

"Whatever it takes, just get us down safely." Raphael's voice oozed barely suppressed rage.

"Yes, sir. You and your wife should strap in. This won't be clean or simple."

Raphael dragged me into a seat just beyond the door and showed me the strapping, making sure I was secure before attending to himself. I made a note to learn so in the future he wouldn't need to forego his own safety for mine.

Then the dirigible started dropping in fits and starts while it creaked and groaned like an ailing ship. In truth, that was exactly what it was, just a ship of the sky, not the ocean.

I could see over the large wheel now, trees obscuring our view, and I hoped we'd find clear ground to land in. I feared that if we came down in a heavily wooded area, the damage to the dirigible might well be irreparable.

The deck jounced beneath my feet, but Raphael's hand was firm, holding mine. I closed my eyes, sure this was the end of everything.

Time passed. My stomach roiled and rose, then fell jerkily.

Suddenly, with a bang, we hit what I hoped was the ground.

Things went flying, glass smashed, and someone—I realised it was probably me—screamed with fright.

A heavy object found its way across the back of my head. Pain exploded, and suddenly it was dark.

* * *

"Francesca, wake up." The voice was frantic as a hand patted at my cheek, clearly attempting to wake me from the horrific dream where my head felt sure to split in two.

Hands tugged at me and dragged straps from my body.

I opened my eyes, and there was Raphael, his face smeared with grime, but it was the terror in his eyes that captured me.

"What's—" I coughed, which made my head feel like it was due to explode.

With careful fingers, I touched the back of my head. Moisture, thick and oozing, coated my fingers. Red. Blood.

"Stay still," Raphael ordered, but I knew what had happened. One look at the bridge told me all I needed to know.

"It was a hard landing."

"God, yes. But you're injured."

I grimaced at his concern. "Just a little. I doubt it's a concussion. My vision is clear, though my head aches, and there's some blood."

He slumped down onto the seat beside me and rested his head in his hands.

I won't tell him anything more in case it panics him further.

"For a moment, you were so still. Pale." He turned to face me and gulped. "I can't... Losing you would tear me apart, Francesca."

I reached out, intending to touch his cheek, but the memory of the smear of blood stopped me short. "Are there any other casualties?"

He just stared at me.

A man raced into the cockpit, his face scratched and grimy, blood oozing from his cut. "Sir, we need assistance in the control room. We got a fire."

Raphael stood and gathered me in his arms.

"Raphael!" I shrieked.

"Hush. I'm getting you off here until I know it's safe."

Chapter Eighteen

I huddled under the blanket, the fire burning hot in a pit quickly put together. Raphael paced like a man consumed.

"Come sit down," I urged.

He looked at me with such pain in his eyes, it hurt to see. "I'm too upset right now."

The guards who remained with us were too close for us to talk freely, but I rose and moved to him.

He sighed and enfolded me in his arms. "They're safe. There are so few accidents that this stands out. Something went wrong." He bit out the words, looking again in the direction of the dirigible.

The captain emerged, his uniform streaked with grime and oils and heaven knew what else. "Well, sir, we found what caused the accident. Someone managed to get an incendiary device—a very small one—into a pressure valve. When it was under load, it blew. That was the initial blast. The damage can be fixed, but it'll take us a day or two. We need to send word to the New York Dirigible Reposihouse. There are some parts we don't have, and they'll be the closest." He looked over his shoulder to the guards, then leaned in close. "It'll take several days for the parts to arrive, leaving us essentially stranded here. And the Marconi was also damaged. I've already got the operator looking into a running repair, but until then, we can't even get the message out."

Raphael slid his hands into his pocket, and while he may have looked from the outside to be calm, I knew a storm was brewing beneath the surface. "What security devices are on board?"

"We have a portable Secura-Fence, and there are two of Mr Whitmore's pantheras."

I blinked. "Pantheras?"

"I thought they were still being tested," Raphael said with a frown.

"They are," the captain said. "He was sending them back to the Whitmore clinic."

"What are they?" I asked both men.

"They're automatons in the shape of a panther. Silent, sleek, and efficient. Your brother Simeon has been working with them for the last six months." My husband turned to the captain. "You have the safeguard settings?"

The captain nodded. "Yes, they were to be delivered to the senior Mr Whitmore's house guard."

"Then deploy them. Set up the security fencing. I want everyone on board come nightfall, but with human guards on the decks. How long do you think the operator will take to get the Marconi working again?"

The captain's face fell. "He says it'll take what it takes. He's the only person we have aboard with that kind of knowledge. But we do have a small datascreen. It doesn't have the capacity to send out, as you know, but we can receive and intercept transmissions. He's been working on that first, so if someone is looking for us—"

"We'll hear about it. Very good. The fire is out, then, I take it?" I interrupted.

"Yes it is, Dr Nobel."

"Then I plan to go aboard, have a shower, and rest for a while." I dragged the blanket around myself and marched forward, leaving the two men watching me.

Once on board, the emotional starch that was holding me up seemed to dissipate, and I wanted to slump to the ground. My head ached, and my body stung in a number of locations, either from the landing or the rolling on the deck, finding every bump possible.

I made it to the bedroom and started tugging at my clothes, nothing more than a shower in mind, when I stopped. It could have been instinct or something more, but I approached the bathroom slowly. If someone had managed to get a small incendiary device aboard the ship in our brief time in New York, what else might they have done?

I closed my hand over the door handle and turned it slowly.

Pushed it open.

A sound echoed within, and I threw myself to the side as the bang filled the air. Smoke, thick and choking, wafted into the air, and I instinctively tugged the material of the blanket over my nose and retreated to the hallway. I screamed, though it was muffled by the material. I yanked the bedroom door shut, following the urging of intuition.

Footsteps came toward me, and I glanced back. Raphael was running, followed by the captain. "Francesca?"

"In—" I coughed. "In the bathroom. Smoke." I coughed again, my eyes watering and burning, the skin of my hands prickling. I glanced down and noted they were red. "I need my bag," I croaked.

Raphael made for the door.

"Wait!" I turned to the captain. "Do you have a flight facemask? A set with goggles?"

He nodded. "We use the in-flight sometimes, when the men have to remove the weather screens."

"Get them, and be quick. Raphael, you'll need that and gloves. Don't go in without them or you'll burn your skin like mine." The red of my skin was turning itchy, and I knew the next phase would be the formation of blisters. "I'm reacting to the chlorides in the smoke." It was seeping into the hall, and I urged him back. "We'll need to open the windows to let it disperse, and everything within will need laundering immediately before we wear or use it."

I coughed again. "Bring my bag. I have an inhalant that will settle my throat and lungs. There's also a cream which will ensure the blisters don't become septic."

Fear flashed across his face. "Blisters?"

"Next phase in the body's reaction to the chloride. I'll be fine in a few days. Just need to let my skin heal."

The captain returned with a flight suit, and Raphael divested himself of his coat and pants inside the cabin nearest the lounge, then returned. The suit barely fit but would do the job. He donned the goggles, then settled the flight mask over the top. He tugged on the weather gloves, and I urged the captain back as Raphael entered the room. Moments later, he emerged with my bag and a grim look on his face.

As Raphael stripped out of the emergency mask, I opened the bag, my fingers stinging. "Did you get the window open?"

He nodded. "Yes. I also looked in the bathroom. It was rigged so that as soon as we opened it, we'd be clouded in the gas." He turned to the captain. "Get the room cleared out. Every piece of clothing, material, and even the carpets will need to be stripped. My wife and I will need clean clothing immediately, so have that attended to first."

When Raphael turned back, he scooped up my bag and ushered me into the cabin. "Bathe first?"

I nodded. "As soon as I've got the inhalant."

"What's it called?"

I rattled off the name, and he settled me in the bathroom as he dug though my bag and found the item. I took it and made quick use of the compound, breathing a little easier. Then he helped me to undress and drew a tepid bath.

I sank into the water, and he grabbed a jug.

"What are you planning to do?" I asked.

"I'll wash your face and hair."

I lay back against the edge of the tub. No one had ever done something like this before, yet it felt right and comforting.

He dipped the jug into the bath. "Close your eyes."

I did as instructed, and the water flowed down my skin, soothing much of the itch. When I was done, he was ready with a bath sheet, which he wrapped around me.

"I can do this," I muttered.

"Yes you can. But for now, let me assist you, Francesca."

He dried my skin, then ushered me into the bed. Once I was swaddled, he took up position on the side of the bed. "Cream?"

"What? Oh." I looked at my hand. The blisters hadn't yet formed. "Calamine. There's a jar."

He moved to the bag, dug out the blue bottle, and dipped his fingers in after removing the lid. With great care, he slathered it on my affected skin with gentle movements.

"I must look a fright now," I muttered.

"Never. Maybe slightly lilac at this point, but never a fright. I'll go see about a cup of tea and will return post-haste."

He rose from the bed, and I fancied he hesitated for a moment. "Raphael?"

As he slowly turned, I considered how to thank him for every bit of care and concern he'd shown me. "Thank you," I croaked.

His brow creased. "Not that I've managed much, but you're welcome."

The door closed behind him, and I exhaled wearily.

Chapter Nineteen

The pantheras proved effective three nights later. Raphael and I were drinking coffee in the lounge when a tremendous roar broke through the air. We both shot to standing, our drinks sliding on the tabletop, and hurried to the door.

The captain beat us to the entrance, and we followed him down the gangplank. I noted the bouncing movement of the mobile incline beneath our rapid pace.

"Let me go!" a man squealed, his collar gripped in the meaty hand of one of the guards.

The security net sparked and buzzed while a panthera stood by, eyes flashing an impressive violet in the growing darkness.

Several other men carrying phosphoric lanterns hovered around, illuminating the scene.

The captain strode forward. "Who are you?"

"I'm no one," the intruder cried, wrenching his body left and right in an attempt to escape his captor.

"You cut through the fencing. You came with purpose. Tell us, or I'll lock you in our guardhouse with a panthera to keep you company."

The intruder's eyes bugged out, and his fear was a palpable stink in the air as he eyed the automaton contraption. "I was s-sent by Mr Nobel. He has a message for you all." He tried to slide his fingertips into the pocket of his coat. He was grizzled and appeared at least forty or older, with grimy grey-streaked hair and heavy growth around his jaw. His face was scarred and battered like he'd lost a million fights with a prize boxer.

"Still!" The snarl came from Raphael, who stalked over. "Have you checked his pockets yet?"

The guard shook his head. "Not yet, sir."

Raphael slid his hand in and quickly tugged it free, revealing a small box. We came closer.

The guard grunted. "Better give that to the captain, sir. It's an incendiary device, like the one found in the valves."

The intruder paled. "It's got a message inside it," he said. "I'm just —" He gurgled, and I stepped forward.

"You're cutting off the oxygen to his lungs. Settle him on the chair. We should tie him up until you decide what you wish to ask."

Eyes turned in my direction, and the guard wavered.

Raphael nodded. "Gag him too."

We stepped aside as the guard set about his task.

"Could it have a message inside?" I felt silly for asking, but not knowing was only part of the problem.

"Perhaps, but seeing the damage wrought by the incendiary, then the smoke bomb in your bathroom, it occurs to me that trusting anything this man has to say may very well be dangerous," the captain answered.

"We might as well have a beacon out here. The sooner we're airborne again, the sooner we can get home and rely on the information from sources we know." Raphael dragged a hand through his hair. I knew he worried about our safety, and my health, given the persistent cough I still exhibited, though I understood it was merely a hangover from the smoke inhalation and would pass within days.

"But how did he get here? How did he know where we were?"

The captain and Raphael looked at each other.

Raphael stepped away, tugging on the gag on the intruder's face. "How did you get here? No one heard any engines."

The man jerked away from the menace in Raphael's words.

"How?" Raphael snapped.

I watched, rapt. Every instinct said he wouldn't hurt the man unless necessary, but that voice... It sent chills through me.

"I... Horse. I rode in and tied it up. Just beyond the lights."

Without a word or even signal, two of the guards tugged their weapons from their backs, the bandoliers slung around their waist and shoulder holsters filled with what appeared to be cannisters. I knew that each of those was a filled cartridge for the fusillade weapons they now carried in their hands. A third man, a crew member, stepped forward and took up a phosphorescent lamp, and the trio walked out beyond the fencing.

Raphael bared his teeth. "Take him to the secured room and lock him in. But check his pockets, boots, and his clothing for anything that could create more difficulties. Then get back here. Leave one on guard, but they are not to talk to him."

The guard nearest grunted a "Yes, sir," then picked up their prisoner and marched him indoors.

"How long till the repairs can be completed, Captain?" The crew from the Reposihouse had arrived this afternoon, and while I knew that was one less concern for Raphael, I was chafing at the restrictions placed on me.

"Tomorrow, if the men are able to fit the new capacitors and the damage to the plasmium cases don't require re-smithing," the captain answered. "It's very tricky to know until the parts are in place if we'll need that. Re-smithing will slow us down by a day or two."

The guards who'd gone beyond the barriers returned, along with a horse being led by its halter.

"Check the saddlebags, plus the saddle itself. Anywhere a transmitter could be concealed, or notes."

I wandered over, well aware that Raphael watched me. "This isn't a living horse. It's an automaton," I warned after feeling a stray prong wheel on the neck while rubbing it.

"Really? You're sure?" Raphael seemed surprised. I took his hand and laid it against the coat. His fingers slid until he found the anomaly. "Indeed. High quality. Not something a stray courier would have on hand."

I shook my head. "No. I vaguely remember Simeon saying he'd

heard something about…" I stepped back. "It should be returned outside the barrier." I hoped they understood the authority in my tone as I headed for the gangplank.

Simeon and Sampson were both well trained in dealing with automatons. They'd be able to answer the question burning inside my head.

I hurried to the Marconi, pleased the issue with the machine was merely a wire needing replacing.

Urgent. Simeon. Sampson. Horse automaton appeared. Remembered conversation. Need details.

I bit my lip, hoping that would be enough to twig their memory. Moments later, a reply came.

Created by Casa Bonita. Lifelike automatons, dangerous depending on mechanical integration. Current utilisation specialised by government. Early prototype disappeared. Whispered to have been in hands of Travis Haven III.

My gut roiled.

I looked up as Raphael joined me in the Marconi room, and I passed him the tape, watching as his face blanched upon reading the message. "Haven. Damn it all."

"We need to know who's in holding. If it's Haven…"

"He has an automatronic arm," I finished for him.

"Can it break through—"

"Maybe. I don't have access to his records, but I'd think… We should get down to holding. But if we stop by our chamber on the way, I have a sedative. It might be best—"

"To return to your father? I agree."

We both hurried up the hall. In our room, I grabbed the sedative and an injector, realising this could be the only safe way to transport our prisoner. If I could get close enough.

"I wish I had a tranquiliser gun at times like this."

"What? Why do you want…?" His brow cleared, and he smiled.

"Oh! Well, there's one in the guardroom. We carry them for animal attacks."

I shook my head. "I should have known you'd have everything and more besides."

Trailing him down the hall to a door at the far end, concealed so it appeared to be part of the wainscoting, I watched as he slid the door open, then followed him into a small room. "Now you know where this is, if you need…" He spread his hands wide.

"Not normally, thank you. But I will remember."

He reached into a cupboard at the back wall and grabbed up a large rifle and a dart. "We haven't much call for using them, but if we get that dart filled with an initial dose, then you can decide once we've immobilised him if it's sufficient."

I bit my lip. "What kind of injector have you included?"

He frowned. "The gun itself releases the dart using kinetic energy, which pressurises the dart containing the drug of choice. The needle is capped to hold the drug in, but once it strikes the target, the cap is pierced by the needle when it punctures the skin."

"Well, that should do the job, then. Help me load it." I checked the amount of solution based on what I guessed was his weight before handing the rifle back to Raphael. "That should be enough, but I'll bring the bottle with me just in case."

We left the room, taking care to close the door behind us. "Don't want him accidentally tripping across this if he does get out," Raphael muttered.

He took me to the end of the hall, through the crew access door, down a set of metal steps that looked rather like a glorified ladder, and then we turned to make our way down a second set.

We hurried down the long white painted corridor, finding the "Secured Room" sign hanging askew. I glanced at Raphael and could almost feel the fury rolling off him. He shunted the door open, and there on the floor lay his man, eyes open but clearly dead.

In the cage, we disturbed our intruder using his artificial arm to bed the bars. Raphael raised the gun as the man I guessed to be Travis Haven roared and reached through.

Bang!

The echo of the gunshot took me by surprised, and I blinked rapidly.

Travis Haven smiled for a moment, then realised it wasn't a bullet. The dart was in his flesh arm. Haven's eyes rolled toward it, and he pulled it out.

"You're too late, Travis. That was a sedative." I stepped closer, but Raphael blocked my way.

"He's still dangerous," he warned.

"Perhaps," I said, then looked up and down the man who wanted me dead. "But we'll have the last laugh. We found your horse. And your good friend Edward Nobel? His membership of SELED and the legal status of Nobel Crest are about to be stripped."

His eyes glinted with hatred even as the power of the drug made its way through his system. "You won't win, little girl. I've got friends. Ones in high places. Much higher than Marcus Bloom." Then he slumped to the floor.

"What does he mean, Raphael?"

My husband turned to face me. "I don't know. But we'll find out. Is he out?"

I slid my hand between the bars, more than aware of Raphael's concern. "It appears so." I stood and moved to the dead man on the floor. No pulse. Closing his lids over sightless eyes, I sighed. "So pointless. The whole thing."

I moved into Raphael's arms, felt the warmth and reassurance of his embrace.

"I would spare you this," he murmured.

"I know. It's just one of the many things you do that make me feel safe and... loved." I'd had days to consider my emotions. Tonight, I felt he needed to hear them. No matter if he returned them or not.

He dragged me close. "Your timing could be improved," he growled against my ear, and as incongruous as it might have been, I laughed.

"I'm aware of that." Tugging away, I met his gaze. "I've been tussling it over for days, since the incident with the smoke. The caring way you looked after me. It..." I shrugged. "I do love you, Raphael."

He cupped both my cheeks and brought our foreheads together so they touched lightly. I felt the exhalation that emerged between his lips.

"I love you too, Francesca. My plan was to arrange dinner back at the house. To make a grand declaration."

"I'm not sure grand declarations are either of us, are they? But what happens now? I mean, we have Travis Haven in our custody."

"If anything he said is correct—and I have no reason to believe he would lie about this—then this is merely the beginning. Haven House was a lesser member, but Nobel Crest was like a jewel. Only one sits above it."

He tensed. I felt the moment the truth—whatever it might be—became apparent. "Which is?"

"Casa Bonita."

The bottom fell out of my world, because that horse out there was a construct of the house. If that was the case... "I see what he means. We need connections. Otherwise, we're on the wrong side of this mess."

The captain chose that moment to come bounding toward us. "The men have checked the casing. They believe they should have the replacements fitted without needing to smith it."

"Can they work through the night?" Raphael's demand was brusque, but now I understood the urgency.

"They could, if necessary," the captain answered.

"Our lives may depend on it."

Chapter Twenty

Landing back at the house, seeing my family again, felt surreal. That we'd been here recently but now I returned as a married woman was only part of the changes. The guards led Travis Haven, looking even more scruffy and untidy than before, into the yard.

Ammy stilled and stared.

Damien approached, his face settled in harsh planes of fury.

"Damien, he's lightly sedated at the moment," I told him. "He's quiet, but I need access to the infirmary in town."

His gaze settled on me, a question blooming.

I glanced away, then back, hating what I was about to say. "I need to remove the automaton replacement. That will allow us to keep him safely under lock and key. Anything less than that and I don't think we have anything strong enough."

After that, I'd release him into Raphael's keeping. He'd already informed me that Marcus Bloom would be arriving in the next day or so.

Damien scanned me. "You're sure?"

I shook my head. "I gave an oath to protect and heal. Sometimes that means removing tissue that will kill the patient. Sometimes it means protecting others. That's my aim. That's what I'll do."

I'd spent the last few days considering it, then planning for the operation. I'd made notes in my journal. "I need Louisa and Miles, though. And some tools I doubt I can access here. Can we send for them?" I turned to Raphael.

"I thought you might need them. They've been on standby for the last few days."

"Then I'll send them a message through the datascreen in Damien's office." Before I retreated, I stepped up to Ammy and encircled her in my arms. "It's good to be home," I said, and she smiled, if a little wanly. I made a mental note to check her again this evening, then headed for the house, well aware that Raphael would explain our adventures to Damien.

Inside, the house was cool and quiet. After the sound of the dirigible motor whirring day and night, the silence was welcome. The *Lady Anthea* would also undergo urgent repairs, as while the work done onsite at our heavy landing might hold, it wasn't what anyone would call reliable.

In Damien's office, I lowered myself to the chair, slid out the concealed unit, and started it up. It hummed, and the oddly shining light at the side of the unit told me it was warming through.

When a ping echoed, it was ready. The keyboard was clunky, with buttons attached to arms, but it was faster and more reliable than a Marconi unit.

I tapped the message out quickly.

Louisa and Miles required urgently at Haven. Tools for replacement of limbs required. Bring the kinetoscope camera, my personal ocular, and the hermetic sealant powder. FN

The grainy picture slid in and out of focus, but I waited, knowing that as soon as the message was received, there'd be a reply. It came quickly.

L&M will arrive tomorrow. On standby already, awaiting your request. Tools and equipment will be collected and transported with them. Reggie

"Good. Then all I need to do is make arrangements. I wonder though, once the limb is removed, what will we find? The power of that hand is more than I expected," I said to myself.

I turned to the research screen, the movement of the handle affecting it slowly. Once I'd typed in my interest string—"Automaton Limbs, Latest Developments"—I waited.

As always, informative links sprang up, but they were quickly brushed aside as not specific enough or without the background I needed. It was only at the third string of information links that I came across a useful piece of information.

Lores, Alveraum (1845-present) Undertaking extreme rebuilding of artificial limbs for the purposes of extending the manual labour capabilities of the wearer. The Lores theory includes replacement of prong wheels with an ionic exchange unit, to increase the mass the patient can lift. Some discussion to the negative has arisen due to the possibility of military use. Alveraum Lores has been struck from the physiotraducere and medical boards as of February 1877 and is forbidden to practice indefinitely. Current whereabouts, Casa Bonita.

I closed my eyes. Casa Bonita. We kept coming back to the one house with the power and resources to derail our work of overcoming the scourge of the cults and releasing the women from servitude.

A knock at the door broke my introspection. Looking up, I watched as Raphael entered, closed the door, and stepped up to me.

"Amaryllis and Damien have put us in the guest wing. I think they're concerned we may need privacy." His smile died away. "What have you found?"

I sighed. "I contacted Reggie. Miles and Louisa will be here tomorrow, along with my equipment and the items I requested. But while I was at it, I ran a short research scan on super-strength in the field of artificial strength in an automatronic limb. It leads back to Alveraum Lores. I didn't know of him before, but if he's doing what's been posited, then he's not just dangerous, he's breaking every rule we have."

I stepped away and allowed Raphael a look at the screen. "And that makes sense, given the horse and everything else we've learned."

My nod was slow. "Yes. Once I've got the arm secured, I intend to have a good look at it. Maybe Simeon and Sampson will be able to shed light on what he's created."

Raphael nodded. "Fine. We'll do that. But for now, let's go bathe and prepare for dinner."

I quirked my brow at him. "At three in the afternoon?"

His grin turned wolfish. "Well, a rest wouldn't do either of us any harm."

I laughed and rose from the console. "I would guess not. But what about Ammy and Damien?"

His lips twitched. "I think they've gone for a rest too."

I pinked, not having really thought about my adoptive parents and the things I'd been doing with Raphael. It was... rather embarrassing. "I'm not sure that's a mental image I appreciate."

He reached out a hand, and I took it. "They said you'd know where our chamber was, in the guest suite."

"I do indeed."

I led Raphael up the stairs, and instead of turning left, we moved to the right-hand side hallway. The bedroom set aside for couples lay at the end of the long hallway, and I was grateful for that. After all, if we got loud, no one would hear us.

Inside the room, Raphael gathered me close. In the days since the explosion, he'd deemed me too fragile for that kind of action, so instead the nights had passed with me snuggled in his arms. Tonight, I had no intention for that to continue.

My fingers toyed with the buttons of his coat. "I do feel, given the weather, that you're overdressed, sir."

"Indeed, wife. Then we should make haste to overcome that, shouldn't we?"

His hands trailed to the buttons, popping each so slowly that I almost ached to reach out and brush his hands aside. My mouth dried as his gaze caught mine and he shrugged out of the fabric, the cambric of his shirt the only covering over his deliciously masculine chest. One I adored sliding my fingers over.

"Wife, it seems you need assistance too." That familiar rumble against me heightened my awareness of my body's reaction.

With knees now turning weak, and the heat flaring deep inside my abdomen, I turned so he could reach the many buttons.

"I can usually handle them myself," I whispered.

"Yes, but today, this is my treat. Uncovering flesh that only I've seen and touched. Knowing that once I've unwrapped my prize, I can engage in acts of carnal enjoyment with you. How could I do anything other than act as your lady's maid?"

I giggled. "You make me sound like a candy."

He kissed the nape of my neck. "Aren't you?"

I arched my back, enjoying the sensuality of the moment, knowing that soon I'd be naked. We'd touch skin to skin, and my body would flame.

He turned me once my dress dropped to the floor. I was clad only in my undergarments, yet I felt no shyness. We were married, and this was the path to a pleasure I'd had no clue existed. Not before him.

"That shirt. It has to go, husband," I whispered breathlessly.

"In that case, will you assist me?"

I found where it had been tucked into his trousers, but my hand touched his belt and pure devilry rose. I took a moment and unhooked it. "Now, then, what comes next?" I murmured, then reached to the buttons of the placket and popped them one by one.

When Raphael's trousers gaped, I pushed them, and they slid down his legs. "Much improved." His heavy erection couldn't be ignored. It jutted against his simple white short cotton drawers, and oh, how I wanted the pleasure it promised.

Raphael's hands settled on my shoulders and turned me so I once more faced away. Then they moved to my laces, and I felt the tugs as he slid them free from the eyes until my petticoat dropped away. "Too many damn layers," he muttered.

I laughed and dragged it from my body. The long chemise followed suit, and I turned, hands plucking at the ties of my bloomers. He'd already shucked his undergarments, so finally we were naked.

I shivered as the caress of air passed over my exposed body, but I didn't shield myself. His eyes roamed. Instead of embarrassment, I felt womanly, wanted, and empowered. Reaching out, I ran a finger down the valley in the centre of his chest. "You feel so good," I whispered.

"Not as good as you will soon."

Raphael advanced, wrapping his arm around my waist and tugging me closer, and I hissed at the feeling of skin against skin. Electricity arced between us, drugging my senses so my eyelids slid down.

"No. Watch. Look." The throatiness in his voice was yet another arousing aspect I couldn't deny that ran between us.

Stepping back and away, I smiled, crooked a finger, and headed for the bed, but he captured me before I could get too far.

"Not yet, my fire. Come. See. Learn." He tugged me toward the long looking glass. I caught sight of our bodies, his looming behind me. My arousal notched up again as he moved his hand over me and captured a breast, held it as if weighing it in his hand, and smiled.

I swallowed, staring as his thumb pressed the nipple, and arched back against him.

"More yet, my love. Keep watching."

He allowed his hand to slide down, and I looked on, mesmerised by the scene unfolding. His hand splayed across my belly. "Soft." He kissed the nape of my neck.

It was torture keeping my eyes open, but I watched as the hand now trailed lower, found the curls hiding my most secret place.

"You open like a petal, soft and damp. Ready." The tips of his fingers glided between the folds of my sex, and I writhed, needing more.

His erection poked at me, and I reached back. My hand folded around him, and he hissed.

"Two are able to play the game," I teased.

"Temptress," he muttered, and I ran my hand along his length.

Now when I turned to him, there was a change in our actions. Instead of lush and slow, the movements became frantic. Our mouths mashed together as he feasted.

Hard fingers gripped my hips, and I was lifted as he dragged his mouth away, "Wrap your legs around me." When I did, I found to my satisfaction that I'd opened for his questing length.

He carried me to the bed, but before he could release me to the coverlet, my body reacted instinctively, flexing, and he slid deep, fully embedded inside me.

"Raph... Raphael," I stammered.

He laid me on the bed, pushing me back so my breasts jutted upward. "Beauty," he whispered and leaned forward, looming over me. Every move was part of the thrust and parry of love. He slid forward; I cried out. His hands found my breasts, plucked at them with a gentleness belying our hunger, and his face tightened, as did the invisible coil inside me, the one that ratcheted up under his ministrations.

The rhythm increased, my pulse pounding, and I reached out, caressing him. "Raphael, please."

He smiled. "For you, my fire. Only for you."

The tempo increased again, urgency rising.

I wanted more. Needed more. Needed that exquisite release he promised. Then I was there, my body shaking and sweaty, and down I fell, into that well of pleasure.

My breathing slowed, my body relaxing as he slumped over me. I ran my hand over his damp flesh, more than aware that he'd been with me the whole way. I'd felt the moment his body released its seed.

Tears welled, not of sadness or horror but in recognition of the gift he'd given me. Himself, without impediment or evasion.

"I love you," I whispered.

His hand languorously found a lock of hair and slid it from my face as he glanced up. "Just as I love and adore you, my fire."

"Why do you call me that?"

He smiled, though it was a little sad. "My father always called my mother that. He loved her. She loved him. I remember this one time, he said to me that if he'd had just a single wife, if his life had gone the way he intended, she'd have been his only. They were devoted."

I wanted to ask more, but it wasn't the time or place. I simply wriggled over. "Come," I said, patting the bed, though I felt sleepy now in the post-loving afterglow.

He climbed onto the bed beside me. "You want to know more. I know that look now." He laughed, then sobered. "My father was the second son. His brother had been groomed to take over. Father never wanted that life, but his brother died shortly before their father, so my father was all there was. My grandparents weren't happy but accepted that there was no other option. Instead, he gave an undertaking that he'd love and adore and protect mothers and their children. That he'd free the house before he died. He did... But Edward, he never wanted that. He coveted the wives, the money. The lifestyle."

Safe in Raphael's arms, I frowned and considered his words. "And his heir is...?"

Raphael slumped back onto the pillows, slinging an arm over his face. "Francesca..."

"It's you, isn't it?" Suddenly so much made sense. It was like a punch to my stomach. "Tell me you're not going to have to..." I couldn't finish the sentence. Instead, I felt the urge to vomit. I had to work hard to contain the contents of my stomach.

"No! I promised you—"

"Like your father?" Tears burned, and I pulled away, suddenly chilled.

"I'm not my father. Once I have the house deregistered with SELED, all will be well." He rolled, sitting up on one elbow. "Trust me."

How I wanted to, but he'd not told me he was the heir. I'd somehow expected it to be Ellis, since Raphael wasn't living at the house, but the enormity of it terrified me. I couldn't share him. Would rather walk away now—if I could—than live a life where he was with other women.

I crawled from the bed and found my chemise to cover my nakedness.

Raphael frowned. "What? What do you expect me to do?"

"I don't know," I whispered, turning away. "I can't live that way."

"You won't."

"And what if they don't deregister the house? How many years has he had to beget an heir? Each year, each bride, the chances grow slimmer. How many brides has he taken?" I turned, letting him see my terror.

Raphael's skin took on a crimson tinge. "He's got, I think, five."

"And not one of them has given him a child?"

Raphael shrugged. "No. Not wives. But, Francesca, be sensible about it."

The word flashed into my mind like a nitroglycerine explosion.

I reared back. "I *am* being sensible. I know what I will and won't tolerate. I know how I lived as a child." Every word hissed out of my mouth. "I won't live like that, nor will I raise a child in that environment." I wrapped my arms around my middle, warding off any further discussion. "Please. I need to be alone."

He paled. "Don't do this, Francesca."

I shook my head. "Please, go." I stalked to the bathing room, shut the door, and turned the key, then settled on the floor to weep.

Chapter Twenty-One

By the time dinner was ready, I'd composed myself. After all, Raphael would, no doubt, be at the table. I needed to ensure neither Ammy nor Damien were aware that I was devastated.

Making my way down the staircase, I kept my head high. In the dining room, I settled in my usual spot and watched as everyone trooped in. That was when the shoe dropped. There was no empty spot.

"Damien? Where did Raphael go?" I tried my utmost to keep the surprise from my voice, but he must have noticed something awry.

"He was upset when he left in the *Lady Anthea* about an hour ago. Said he had unfinished business."

The trembling started in my hand, becoming a clatter of spoon against bowl before I stood. "Please excuse me. I... I need to be excused." I was out of the chair and moving swiftly for the door as the tears started streaming.

I hadn't expected him to *leave*!

"Damn you, Raphael," I sobbed and dropped to my knees in the drive. I didn't care who saw me. What I wanted? I had no idea, but it wasn't Raphael leaving me here.

A hand slid over my shoulder. Ammy.

"Francesca, tell me what's wrong, dear." I heard the concern in her voice, but it only made me sob harder.

She waited until the convulsions of grief passed, then helped me to stand, enfolding me in her arms. "What happened?"

"I... We fought, Ammy. He didn't tell me he was Edward's heir. I assumed, since he was free to marry, that it was Ellis."

"Oooohhh... He must take another wife?"

I shrugged, then shook my head. "I don't know. I mean, he said he had no intentions to do, but that's what his father had said initially. But when Adam's died, he had to assume the house and had no choice, even though he had a wife." I rubbed at my aching eyes. "I'm so confused. I didn't expect him to leave, Ammy."

"You think he's left you for good? That doesn't seem like the kind of thing Raphael would do."

I laughed. "I guess I don't know him as well as I thought. Nor do you." I turned back, gazing at the spot where the dirigible had rested. Wishing he was still here. Wishing we could talk.

You could have talked, but you sent him away, remember?

My throat ached, and I sighed. "What do I do now?"

She smiled sadly. "I think all you can do is give him time. Stay busy and focussed."

I nodded slowly. "I'm not very hungry. I might just retire."

Ammy rubbed my shoulder. "I'll send a cup of tea up. Go change and climb into bed. I'll be along soon."

I moped my way inside and up the stairs, turning to the room we'd been meant to share, feeling very alone.

Stripping out of my gown, I donned the night-rail I'd not worn since my wedding night and climbed into bed as the door opened. Ammy limped in with her maid shadowing her, carrying a cup of tea and a beaker of something else.

"Just a simple decoction. It'll calm your nerves and help you sleep," Ammy said and pressed it into my hands.

I drank it down, even though the bitterness cut through the honey sweetener. Then I took the cup of tea.

"Ammy?" I said softly.

"Hmm?"

"I love you."

She caressed my cheek. "I know. You're a treasure to me. All of you are. Now rest easy. Sleep, and in the morning, perhaps we'll know more and have a better perspective on what he's doing and where he's going."

They left the room, and I settled in the large bed. I could still smell the scent of musk, faintly now but enough that my heart ached. I took the pillow he'd laid his head on, hugged it to my chest, and hoped that I'd not destroyed everything with my anger.

* * *

"Francesca! Come quick. He's waking, and we need to sedate him again."

I rolled up the sleeves of my gown and entered the cell where we were holding Travis Haven.

Two full days had passed since Raphael left. I'd stayed busy, making arrangements for the surgical procedure. With Miles and Louisa by my side, I was prepared for today. I didn't expect it to be easy, but at least I now had all my tools.

His eyes opened blearily as he lay on the bed. "What you gonna do?" His voice was sloppy from the drugs.

"I'm going to put you under again," I said and held up the syringe.

"Not gonna...," he slurred and tried to bat my arm away, but Miles was there. He held him still until the drugs took effect. We'd been keeping him twilighted, enough to attend to feeding and watering and bodily functions but not enough to use the strength of the automatronic arm against us.

"Bring him through to the operating room. I'm ready to begin," I ordered.

Miles, Simeon, and Sampson carried him in and laid him on the table. Then my brothers retreated to next door. They didn't have the stomach for such procedures, but at least if I needed them, they'd be there.

I checked his sedation levels. "Miles, he's out, but I need you to watch him. If he looks like he's coming around, we'll need an increased dose."

"Yes, Doctor." He also had a cloth and a bottle of chloroform in case I needed to move quickly.

Louisa set my tools beside me, and with a deep inhalation, I began. I inspected the appendage, checking the prong wheels fasteners I was sure held the material that covered the connective points.

Bit by bit, I disassembled the mechanical fitment. First the inner arm, then outer. They slid and slipped, and I wondered at the craftsmanship even as I tugged it apart.

With the first layer removed, the hydraulic system was on display. It took time and attention to find every prong and remove them.

Now all that remained was the skeletal outline and the nerves and tendons they'd attached it to.

I bit my lip and started the incisions.

"Doctor? He's waking," Miles murmured.

I glanced up, then called to Louisa. "Hold these clamps still while we dose him up."

I hurried around and had just taken up the syringe when he moved, mechanical hand reaching for me, the other swatting at Louisa.

Miles grabbed his arm, but not before it made contact with the side of my face. I lurched but thankfully kept the hypodermic in my grip. Then I plunged it deep, pushing down to ensure all the dose was delivered, and hoped I'd been quick enough and the dose was sufficient to push him back to sleep.

As he relaxed, I exhaled in relief. "Well, that was a bit of excitement."

I returned to Louisa and inspected the damage. Thankfully she'd kept the clamp in place so we hadn't had a major blood flow.

Then I took up my scalpel and began again.

Chapter Twenty-Two

The chair called to me, exhaustion sapping the last burst of energy as I cradled the arm in my hands. It was heavy, exceptionally well crafted, and dangerous.

I'd barely missed the syringe embedded in the skeletal makeup—a failsafe, I guessed. The double point assured me it was meant to be equally as effective on both patient and physiotraducere.

Louisa and Miles were keeping an eye on Haven, but he'd be returning to his cell soon enough, when my brothers returned. They'd headed off to track down some food for the three of us. The clock on the wall told me I'd been at it for four and a half hours. Not a long time in the usual scheme of removals, but it had been tricky.

If Lores was the architect, he'd done an exceptional job, not just of designing but also installing it.

A bang on the door echoed, and I raised my head. "Who is it?"

No one answered, so I rose, placing the arm on the chair, and went to investigate.

I'd yet to remove my bloodstained apron, but I was simply too tired to care.

Looking out the door, I saw no one. I scanned sideways, both ways. No one. Perhaps someone was playing a trick.

Miles came out. "Who's there?"

I shrugged. "I don't think anyone is out there. We should get Travis into his cell though. Don't want him waking on the table."

"No, I doubt that would be a good idea. He might be in poor condition, but he's still as strong as an ox."

I smiled at Miles's comment. "Indeed. I think, with the three of us, we could manage." We stepped into the theatre and hefted the patient, taking great care to avoid holding the arm I'd operated on.

As Miles had indicated, he was heavy, and we moved in fits and starts with several grunts along the way. It felt like it took forever, but once we'd settled him on the bed, I took a last look at his eyes. "He'll be out for a little longer." Then we left the cell, which I locked before handing the key to Miles.

Louisa had prepared the basins, and plunged my hands into the warm water. Cleansing after an operation was an important ritual. First, I let my hands soak before taking up the soap and lathering freely. Then I rinsed, dried, and hoped Louisa had arranged a coffee for me.

As soon as I sat down with the cup in hand, the bang happened again. I made to rise.

"Stay here. I'll take a look," Miles insisted.

I let him go, taking the automatronic arm and hefting it. "I'm going to put this out of sight," I muttered and had barely slid it into a box when a crash echoed. I turned to see what was happening, and my breathing seized.

Edward filled the doorway, his face twisted with rage.

Behind him were three men, each more vicious-looking than the last.

"So, dear Francesca," he sneered. "Reduced again to nothing more than a hatchet sawbones."

Jitters took up root in my belly. If Edward was here, that meant... "What have you done to my brothers?"

He smiled, but there was no mirth on his face. "Brothers? Oh, the two lying face down in the alley behind here? Oh, dear, they seem to have come by an accident."

I gulped because Miles lay still on the floor. Louisa halted silently beside me, her face pale and terror roaring through me.

"Edward, I don't know why—"

"Shut up!" His snarl stilled me. Something about the way he spoke, the way he looked at me, spoke volumes on his mental state. Precarious.

I'll need to watch myself. I stepped forward. "Are you looking for Raphael?"

He laughed, the sound a razorblade on my jangling nerves.

"My brother is a traitor. He thought to have my house deregistered. Imagine it, my malleable little brother taking directions from a whore. One who serviced the father, now servicing the son."

The words cut deep, but I had to keep my calm. "Edward, please—"

"My name is Master. From this point on, that's how you'll address me. Once I make you mine, you'll learn to watch your tongue."

His men stepped forward, and Louisa—God bless her soul—tried to shield me. They flung her to the side, and she fell heavily, the crash loud in the sudden silence.

"Louisa!" I cried and lurched in her direction.

Meaty hands grabbed me, pulling me upright and over to Edward.

His hand cruelly grabbed my chin and forced it upward so I looked directly into the path of his madness, his eyes shining, pupils mere pinpricks. "You'll be an addition to Nobel Crest. Yet another submissive wife. Perhaps you won't fail me as the others have." Spittle landed on my face, but I couldn't loosen myself enough to wipe it away.

It took a second for reality to hit, and then I doubled over. I retched on the floor at his feet, and he pushed me away. He intended to bed me —by force if necessary.

Edward raised a hand, a handkerchief covering his nose, as he paled. "Disgusting woman! Take her away. I'll attend to her later."

He whirled and stomped away, and the men dragged me from the clinic. In the distance, I saw a carriage. On the side was the Nobel Crest blaze.

"No," I pleaded, attempting to free myself from their grip. "Please, don't do this." I sounded piteous, but the fear inside me was growing, taking on its own life like a thick black cloud.

It enveloped me. Then darkness gathered me up.

* * *

I slowly returned to consciousness, but I didn't know where I was or how long I'd been insensible. Only that, in that time, I'd been transferred to somewhere pitch black.

I tried to rise but discovered I was contained in what I guessed was a cage, the lid low. I shuffled side to side, attempting to find the boundaries.

The bars were cold, as was the environment I found myself in.

Shivering, I settled down on the floor. Surely someone had to come for me soon. Then I'd learn more. Maybe find a way to escape.

The chill crept into my bones. My teeth chattered.

"Someone. Come find me. Come find me soon," I begged, but the chill only grew deeper.

* * *

I must have dozed, because when I opened my eyes again, I was in a larger cage, infinitely warmer, but now there were other women. One with long straggling hair, dressed only in a light but stained chemise. Another girl—if she was more than fourteen, I'd be surprised—her hair in pigtails but sporting a bruise on her cheek, wearing a light linen shift.

"Where are we?" I rose, moved toward the bars, and grabbed hold. They were grimy, and I wondered how many other women had been in this position.

"Ain't nothing you can do, dearie. He bought us, paid good coin. We're going to his castle." The older one chortled. "A castle? You ever heard such ridiculousness?"

The girl shivered. "I want to go home! Mama sent me for a loaf of bread, but someone put a bag over me. I tried to fight..." She whimpered and knuckled her eyes.

"Where are we?" I asked.

"Don't know," the girl answered.

I bit my lip. "What's your name?"

"Em... Emily," she whispered, and I closed my eyes, wishing I could somehow find a kinetic pistol in my pocket, thereby freeing us both.

"Ain't gonna need a name, missus." The older woman giggled, then lifted a bottle to her lips and swigged. "You're just gonna be another ride, like all us women."

I gasped at the crudeness of the woman's words. "She's a child," I said.

"Ain't no child. Old enough to bear a young. Comely too."

Emily slid down, tears streaming down her cheeks. "I want to go home. Please, help me."

I wanted to. But to help her, I'd have to help myself first. "How long have I been here?"

The woman shrugged. "Just today."

I nodded and tried to make sense of how long I'd been missing.

By now, Damien would know something was wrong. He'd have sent men, and maybe he'd made contact with Raphael. *Surely Raphael isn't still so angry with me that he would refuse assistance?* My guts wobbled at that thought.

A sudden shunt took my attention. Everything around us lurched, and Emily cried out with fear.

"We're on a train?" I couldn't help myself, the words spilling out.

"Yeah. So what?" said the woman.

"Just trying to understand our situation," I muttered, my eyes on Emily, who now rocked back and forth, a wild look in her eyes and her arms wound around herself.

The rattle and clank of the wheels on the rails sped up. I knew something had to happen soon, or I'd be lost. Not prepared to give in, I gripped the bars of my cage and started prowling, looking for a weakness, a clip or even the latch being loose.

My feet, bare now that I looked down, swept over the floor, sawdust coating it. Nothing.

All that was inside the surprisingly large cage was a pallet, blanket, and bucket. It didn't take much to work out what that was for, and though my bladder was definitely bursting, I'd hold off as long as I could.

"What's your name?" I asked the woman drinking freely.

"What's it your business?" she sputtered.

"Please," I answered.

"Lana."

Perhaps if I worked on Lana, she may yet become an ally. I'd need every one I could scrape together if I was going to survive this mess I was in.

"Lana, how long have you been here?"

She cackled. "Long enough to know what's going to happen."

I shrank back from her words, but I could see how much they were affecting Emily.

"Hush, Lana. You don't need to make Emily feel worse," I scolded.

Now Lana laughed. "What are you? A mother hen?"

Anger and terror warred inside me. I had to hold back my instinctive retort, instead resting my forehead on the bars. "Stop, Lana. Stop. You may be resigned to your fate, but Emily and I are not. I'll help you if I can, but Emily and I are going to find a way out of here. Safely. You can join us or not. That's your choice, but stop with the hate."

She slid the bottle down and stared at me. I couldn't tell if it was shock or anger that shut her up. Whichever way, she backed away from the front of the cage to settle on her pallet.

Emily glanced up. "You're going to help me?"

"We're going to help each other, Emily," I answered. "I just don't know how yet."

* * *

They brought the food in. Slop was a better description, but I took it up anyway, thankful for something in my belly. The train had stopped, and I wondered if we were at some siding or if it stopped for the night.

I watched the guard, the way he flirted with Lana, who allowed liberties, and wondered. Could she be persuaded to assist us? I knew she was gruff and coarse, but that didn't mean she, or any of us, had to accept this fate.

When the guard left, Lana chuckled. "Well, if you want out, I have a way."

I stared at her. "What?"

She sighed. "I wasn't always like this." She swept her hand over herself. "I was once a wife and mother. A long time ago." Her face took on a wistful look. "I had a little boy. Cute little thing. They died, and I was left alone, on the street. There was only one thing I was good at, so I used it."

I didn't need her to tell me what it was, but the remains of a pretty woman still lived in the hunted creature of wild hair and bruised eyes.

"I can help you, Lana. Help us out of here, and I'll do everything I can to give you a life with dignity."

Now her eyes carried pools of misery. "And why would you want to help me?"

"Because I can. Once I'm out of here, I'll make contact with my father and mother. I run the Whitmore Foundation. Have you heard of it?"

She sneered. "I asked them for help once. Before my husband died, after he was injured. They didn't answer."

I bit my lip, tears in my eyes. "I will help you."

Lana sighed and closed her eyes. "I ain't got no future, but you and Emily clearly want something else. Get me out of here and—"

"I won't leave you behind. But we need to act soon or else there will be no way back. Please."

She smiled, then hooked her fingers into the valley between her breasts and retrieved a key. Reaching through the bars, she inserted the key, and it turned. She stepped over and released me, then Emily.

"So now what?"

"Where's the door?" I asked.

She smiled. "There's the slider, but it's loud. There's a smaller access one." She pointed to it.

"Good. Let's see where we are."

I turned the knob and opened the door a little at first. Not seeing anyone, I opened it further. A siding. The men weren't in sight, and I exhaled in relief. With careful moves, I slipped out of the train car and squatted down. No feet on the other side.

Raising a finger to my lips, I urged them to follow me. Lana reached up and closed the door so it wasn't obvious we'd escaped. Scrubby bushes dotted the area, and I wondered if they would be sufficient cover. Would they even check on us before the train departed?

We moved slowly, with care, sharp rocks on the ground tearing at the tender soles of my feet. I hissed and gritted my teeth but kept going.

We dropped down behind the bushes, and only just in time, as a man wandered around from the back of the train, inspecting up and over before climbing into the engine car.

The train whistle blew, and then the train started with a shunt and rattle. Several men climbed onto the tops of the carriages, and I sent up a silent prayer that we'd escaped when we did.

We hid for a long time after the train departed before rising. "I'm not sure we'll get much assistance here," I muttered.

"Nah, don't think so," Lana added. "I heard the men saying they'd be stopping at Elkhurst to resupply, and they're pretty friendly with the locals."

What to do? Perhaps I might find a Marconi and I could send a message to Damien. Or do we take a chance and try to walk out? I don't even know where Elkhurst is, and we'd have to follow the tracks, making it easier for Edward's men to find us.

"Now what?" Lana asked.

I turned and looked at her and Emily. "We have two choices. We could look for a Marconi, but we'd need to keep our wits about us. It's my preferred option. Or we walk the tracks, which is dangerous. They'll track back and come looking. Unless we get lucky, and we can't really be assured of that. We could be caught with ease."

Emily started to cry, and I gathered her close.

"I reckon the Marconi," Lana said. "If the men come in, I can keep them occupied. But if I do that, you gotta promise me you'll help when we get out of this jam."

I nodded. "I will. Emily, do you think you could be our lookout?"

The girl swiped at her face and nodded. "Y-Yes."

As far as plans went, it was rather weak, but no plan wasn't an option.

I stood and looked at the small knot of buildings. Marconis were usually situated near transport stations, and this one looked rickety and old. The building itself was little more than a raised shack.

"Emily, we're going to head for that building." I pointed to it. "You get underneath, out of sight. If you hear or see anything, knock on the floors. I'll hear you. Lana, you're with me." I guessed having lived on the streets, she'd likely have some skills at looking after herself. "I'll need someone to watch out for me once I start sending the message." Already my mind was buzzing with the words.

We crept along slowly, the ground hard with sharp rocks, but I bit my lip and kept going. Time was of the essence. I regretted now not checking with Lana if they were likely to check the cages at night or simply wait until morning, but we didn't have the time to stop.

On light feet, I slipped up the steps, shadowing the building as Emily crawled beneath. With Lana following me, I glanced in the window, and elation filled me. A Marconi. Old, probably poorly cared for, but if I could get that message out, we had a chance.

I signalled Lana, and she opened the door. I darted inside, half expecting to find a lout or guard, but none were there.

"See if you can find any weapons while I get the Marconi working," I instructed.

The power connection to the machine was old and battered. I just hoped it had enough to send the message.

Once I was satisfied it was ready, I sent a quick tape.

Taken prisoner, now escaped. At Elkhurst with two others. Need assistance urgently. Dangerous situation. Francesca.

I turned and glanced at Lana, who held up two kinetic pistols and an ancient harquebus.

"Do you know how to use them?" I asked her.

Lana nodded.

"Good. I'll take a pistol, then, and we'll get Emily in here to take the other," I said, then rapped on the floor.

"What?" came the muffled question.

"Come inside quickly."

She must have scrambled, because she joined us within a minute or so.

I saw some jackets on pegs and grabbed them, passing them to Emily and Lana. The night was turning cold, and we'd already suffered enough indignities. "Put these on. Emily, do you know how to shoot?"

She nodded. "A little."

I passed her a kinetic pistol and ran through the basics. "Just make sure to point it away from us, okay?"

She nodded as the Marconi chattered to life.

Coming for you. Stay safe.

My gut clenched. "I just hope they're quick," I murmured.

We settled in a corner, having assigned watches. We needed rest if we were going to survive, because at any time Edward's men might discover we'd escaped and come looking for us. The men from the town might accidentally find us. So many things could go wrong.

Emily settled into a light doze, and I looked at Lana. "Do they usually check during the night?"

She shrugged. "Sometimes. Usually when we've been loud." She smiled, but it was sad. "If the guard realises I have the key, then yes."

"Is that likely?"

She shrugged, and I closed my eyes for a second, wishing luck would be on our side. Thus far she had, but she was also fickle.

Lana took over a couple hours later, and I rested my eyes, not prepared to sleep but at least conserving my energy.

I was turning to get more comfortable when sounds from outside had me shaking Emily awake. I raised my finger to my lips and primed my pistol.

Blood surged in my system as I prepared for whatever would come. I might have been trained to save lives, but I wasn't going to allow that training to overrule my instincts. "If it's Edward's men, we shoot to save ourselves. If it means killing, then so be it." My voice croaked with the strain of the situation, and my fingers trembled on the trigger.

The sound drew closer. A whomping thud.

Dirigible.

"What's that?" Emily asked, pointing to the sight filling the window.

"Hopefully that's help," I muttered, but though my heart jumped, and I hoped it was the *Lady Anthea*. I couldn't be sure, so I had Lana and Emily hang back.

It landed with a thud, and I heard the pantheras' roar and Raphael's bellow. "Francesca!" It was twinned by Damien's, and I exhaled.

"The cavalry," I exclaimed and urged the women to follow me through the door.

"Francesca!" the bellow echoed again in the still air.

"Here," I answered, and we picked our way carefully toward the knot of men—Raphael's men—who were illuminated by the lamps others held aloft.

He ran toward me, grabbing me in his arms, and I closed my eyes because the other half of me, the one who'd left me, held me tight.

Tears burst forth, and my body shook as the fright of the last few days washed over me. Exhaustion and fear crashed down on me now that I was safe in his embrace once more.

Raphael lifted me into his arms and gave orders for Emily and Lana to be herded aboard just as men from the small village came spilling out of their buildings.

"What's going on?" one growled.

I lifted my head from Raphael's chest and glanced up. His face was alive with fury. "We're here to save my wife," he sneered at the villager. "And if you get between us and the women we're sheltering, you won't like what happens."

"You ain't got no authority here," one of the locals yelled in response.

Damien gave the order, and the pantheras padded their way to the front.

The locals' faces filled with terror.

"Raphael," I whispered, and he looked down.

"Hush, my fire."

Those three little words broke me again.

One of the locals lifted a harquebus, and Damien whistled. The lights of the pantheras' eyes started glowing as they prepared to attack.

"We don't want no fight. Take them and go," an older man called. "Not our fight."

"But, Granpa, the man on the train, he said—" the younger man who'd lifted the rifle whined.

"She's his wife, like he says? Then Edward Nobel ain't got no call holding her. We don't want no trouble, sir," he called back.

"Granpa!"

"Hush, you!"

Raphael turned and carried me to the dirigible, and Lana and Emily followed up the ramp and into safety.

Chapter Twenty-Three

Aboard the *Lady Anthea*, Raphael gave orders for Emily and Lana to be escorted to a chamber where they could bathe, and then he'd arrange food for them. Senny, the female cook's assistant, was sent up to help them, which she did without a complaint.

Meanwhile, Raphael carried me to our bedroom. The whole time, I felt him shaking.

Unsure of what he'd say or how he'd react, I kept my mouth closed. To be honest, that he'd come had been an uncertainty that gnawed at me. Now, he held me close and had used the endearment, "my fire."

Once within our chamber, he kicked the door shut, then headed for the chair, still holding me tight. "I thought I'd lost you, Francesca. I've never been so terrified in my life."

His voice shook, and I looked up, noting the sheen of tears and the way his mouth, his firm and enticing lips, wobbled.

"I'm here now," I whispered.

"I almost lost you."

"You'd care? After what happened?"

He glanced away, and when he looked back, misery was painted on his features. "I was headed for the nearest team, determined I'd go track down Edward and have him release me from my responsibilities."

His words stole my breath. "I..."

"I'd do anything for you, Francesca. Anything." Stark honesty coated his words.

"I thought you'd left me."

He sighed. "You were so angry that I couldn't exactly tell you. I was going to leave a message but didn't. I was furious and hurt, but I never intended you to think I'd abandon you."

I sniffed now, trying to hold back the tide of tears. "So you just left?"

"Only to find help." He closed his eyes, and lines, newly etched, bracketed his mouth. "I didn't expect Edward would kidnap you though."

I sat up, my body alert with sudden memory. "But Sampson, Simeon, Louisa, and Miles?"

"Miles was injured but will make a full recovery with time. Louisa broke her arm when she fell. Your brothers both have very hard heads."

I nodded as tears dribbled down my face. "They all tried to save me."

"They did. And meanwhile, Travis Haven committed suicide in the cell. Once he woke and realised what had been done... He was a weakling, Francesca."

I sniffed. "Damn it. I know Father wanted to interrogate him."

Raphael barked a laugh. "As for Damien, he was beside himself. Your father—"

"Ammy?"

"She's tougher than you think. I wouldn't be surprised if she doesn't have the cooks making broths and sustaining meals for you on your return. Your sisters are bolstering her, and we had a private Marconi from Constance, who said, 'Mother will be much happier when you tell us you have Francesca safe.'"

I laughed, and it felt good to be able to throw off my concerns for a few moments. "Constance is strong. She'll find her own way."

"Like her older sister. Now, come." He stood, and I started sliding to the floor. "I'll draw you a bath and—"

"Owww!"

"What?" Fire lit his eyes, and he lifted me once more.

"My feet. I think I've hurt them," I cried.

He settled me on the chair and raised one, then the other. "What the...? What did they do?"

"They took my boots, and we had to run barefoot on the ground. The stones were sharp. Emily and Lana will need their feet attended to."

"After yours have been cared for," he muttered. He took a step, then came back, dropping a scorching kiss on my lips. "I love you, Francesca. Never, ever forget that. You *are* my fire."

He retreated, and I heard him in the bathing room, the rush of water. Then he returned, gathered me in his arms, and carried me to the bathroom. Settling me on the side, he divested me of the stained and sweaty undergarments, which were all I was clad in.

Then, with such care my heart clenched, he lowered me into the bath.

He stayed as I washed, then lifted me up, carried me to the bedroom swaddled in towels, dried my hair, and dressed me, all as if I were a fine china doll.

I let him, because I knew he needed the reassurance as much as I did.

"We need to go find Lana and Emily," I said when he laid down the brush.

"I'll carry you," he offered.

"I'm sure I can walk." I laughed.

"Perhaps, but you're safe in my arms."

I couldn't comment on the safe part, but I did feel loved and sheltered there, so I acquiesced.

He bundled me into the dining room where Lana and Emily waited for me, and food had already been laid out. Damien hovered around as I looked at the table with narrowed eyes. The soft food options turned my stomach, just thinking about the gruel we'd been fed. "Honestly, if there's something else? This is..." I indicated the plates. "I know you've all worked so hard..."

"It's okay. Thanks, Francesca," Emily whispered. "I know why you're saying that. But I'm hungry," she added shyly, so I simply nodded as Mason, one of his Raphael's men watched by the door, ready to pounce into action, I thought.

Lana attacked the bowl in front of her as if she'd not seen food for a long time, and I made a mental note to contact the foundation as soon as we arrived... "Where are we going, Raphael?" I asked.

He grunted, arm still tight around my waist. "Back to your parents' home, initially. Then back to the house in the city. I'll need more men to make any impression on Edward."

"We, Raphael. When *we* take down Nobel Crest."

Damien cleared his throat, and I glanced at him. "About that. Marcus Bloom is making representations, but unless we can prove Edward was involved in the kidnapping we can't act on the abduction."

I frowned. "What about what the boy said in the village?"

He frowned. "Indeed. In the rush, we didn't think about that. Mason? Send for the boy and his grandfather."

Lana and Emily both looked up, and Lana smiled. "Edward Nobel? Bastard that he is, he offered me money for a quick ride, and then his men stuck me in a cage."

Raphael's eyes narrowed, but I squeezed his hand. "Lana is going to seek assistance from the foundation when we arrive back in town. She was ignored when her husband was injured. He and her son died, and she..." I shrugged.

"Forgive me, then, Lana," Raphael apologized. "We'll offer you every assistance. What are your skills?"

I stared at Lana, and she smiled, though there was a whisker of devilry dancing in her eyes. "Sewing."

He nodded. "I'm sure there's plenty of work as a seamstress. Indeed, my wife"—he glanced at me—"has need of an expanded wardrobe. Perhaps you may be of assistance."

Lana's eyes widened with shock. "I... You're offering me work?"

"Of course, the household is really Francesca's purview, but I don't see why we can't find a place for you."

I wanted to remonstrate, but the kindness Raphael was extending was so genuine and heartfelt that I kept my thoughts to myself.

The trip home turned silent as we all retreated into ourselves, considering the nights and days past.

When the house came into view, I cried, held safely in Raphael's arms.

Chapter Twenty-Four

Ammy was indeed waiting in the early light of dawn as the dirigible landed. Raphael refused to let me walk, though Lana and Emily both insisted they would enter the house on their own two feet.

In her gown, with the shawl tugged tightly around herself, if not for the thickening of her waist, I'd think Ammy was still the young girl who'd taken us away from squalor in Haven township. "Oh, Francesca, I was beside myself. Come inside, and bring your friends with you."

She smothered me, and as much as I knew she needed surety that I was safe, all I wanted was to sleep, wrapped in Raphael's arms.

As if he understood my dilemma, he smiled at Ammy. "I think Francesca is exhausted. If you don't mind, it's been a long, hard few days, and we all could do with rest. Perhaps you might find somewhere for Lana and Emily to rest as well?"

"Of course," she said, spreading her arms wide. "Follow me, ladies. You must be desperate to sleep. The dirigibles are fine, but there's nothing like a bed in a house for rest."

Raphael made for the staircase, then turned, looking at Damien, who followed us. "Thank you for your assistance. I can't express—"

"Nonsense. I'm just overjoyed Francesca is safe. But perhaps next time..." He stopped and shook his head. "Later. Go upstairs now. Sleep."

Raphael hesitated, his body tensing, but then he nodded, and I lay quietly in his arms. I would never usually call myself the fainting type of female, but I needed the assurance of his touch right now.

In the bedroom, he set me down. "Does that hurt your feet too much?" He hovered like an expectant father, and I smiled, wanting only to put his mind at rest.

"No, it's fine." I started to strip, and he watched, leaning against the door, his eyes gleaming. I completed the act, aware of the intimacy of my husband standing there, simply watching with a dry mouth. *Will he join me?*

As I was reaching for the nightgown, he pushed my hand away. "Leave it," he muttered and began his own striptease. My body responded, heating and firming. I bit my lip as he finally dropped the last piece of clothing to the floor and advanced.

"Are you...? Do you want this?" The hesitancy of his words hurt.

I nodded. "Yes."

His arms enfolded me, and I sucked in what felt like the first full breath since my abduction.

His mouth settled over mine, and I welcomed him, needing the reassurance. He was gentle, sipping at my lips as I sighed. His hands roamed my body, reacquainting himself, and I followed his actions. Muscles firmed at my touch as I found him, heavy and ready.

I tugged away and climbed onto the bed. "I want you," I said, well aware it was bold to ask for this intimacy.

"Then I shall oblige, my fire."

I hummed at his answer and settled myself against the pillows. He crawled across the coverlet, the body of a hunter, and I was his prey. It excited me so much that I hissed.

He placed his mouth to one thigh, proffering a tender kiss, followed by another, then yet another, each one slightly inching upward.

The closer he came to my sex, the more I quivered as hunger flashed in his eyes.

"Raphael?"

"I want to taste your fire, my love. Be still."

I'd heard of such caresses, but this? It was erotic, the touch of his breath against my skin leaving me trembling and needy. The fire inside me rose as my breasts pebbled with the kiss of the air against sensitive flesh.

I cupped them, feeling the need, and his eyes glinted with arousal. "You are truly the most sensual being I know. Beautiful. Kind. Sexy."

My eyes dropped closed as his mouth opened over me. My body convulsed at the pleasure, and I thought I'd explode, yet each time I approached the point of no return, Raphael stopped.

His hands quested, relearning the dips and hollows, touching me with such exquisite care.

"I want—"

He laughed. "Not this time. Next. When I have more control. If you touch me," he growled, "I'll not last. This time is all for you. Your pleasure."

And pleasure me he did, gliding up my body, caging me yet never exerting a pressure I didn't welcome.

His hard cock nudged and then slid inside me as we kissed and I tasted my own musk.

I writhed against him as he moved and fed the emptiness inside me, and I wanted it all. I wanted his pleasure, his cries. My legs circled his hips, and the tempo increased until our joint orgasm crashed down upon me, swallowing us both.

* * *

I lay sprawled across him, unsure how that had happened but welcoming the intimacy.

"How did you escape?" he asked.

I briefly described what had occurred while his hands kept up a steady movement of tracing circles on my skin.

"You're incredibly resourceful, my fire. When we have Edward in hand—"

"What will you do? As the heir, you have a responsibility to the house."

He sighed. "The information we were able to give Marcus should encourage the board of SELED to remove Nobel Crest from the register. We have witnesses. You, Lana, and Emily along with Jed and his grandson. More than enough. Along with Miles's testimony and Louisa's and those who caught sight of them…"

"Who else?"

"Members of the community. Those with standing. The mayor, for one."

"When will you know?"

"That's always hard to know. If they convened straight away, there should be enough to urge them to move." He shrugged. "But for now you should sleep."

A tremendous yawn escaped. "I don't want to, but—"

"Listen to your body. What it needs. I'll still be here when you wake."

I cupped his jaw. "I was wrong to lose my temper with you. I said things—"

"Nothing has been simple for us, Francesca. Nothing has gone to plan, and if I had my way, we'd be back at the mansion, working on making a baby."

I stopped, arrested by that thought. "You wish for—"

"When the time comes, I would welcome yours. A child made by us."

I smiled, wondering if we'd already achieved that. I'd know in time. Instead, I cuddled in and allowed sleep to claim me.

* * *

I woke to the touch of his lips upon my brow. "Wake up, my fire. I have news."

My eyelids felt heavy, but I opened them anyway. "Raphael?"

"Marcus Bloom has sent word. They deregistered Nobel Crest. They've seized the assets and will be handing them into my care."

That wakened me, and I sat up. "What? When?"

"He'll meet us at Nobel Crest. His own men, Damien's, and ours will travel with us."

I shook my head, trying to urge the last vestiges of sleep to depart. "When do we leave?"

"Immediately. He's going to hold off Edward until we arrive." Raphael urged me up, and I rose, reaching for the clothes he'd already found for me.

"He's there?"

"Bloom says so. Said the train arrived late last night, but there was a ruckus given the carriage was empty." He smiled, but the light in his eyes was full of malice. "When we arrive, my brother and I will have words."

I bit my lip and dressed in silence as I tossed over the realities of how much Edward's actions had hurt him.

Raphael must have seen my concern, because he reached out and kissed the knuckles of left my hand. "He has to pay, Francesca. Has to know and understand that what he did was wrong. Hideously so."

I nodded. "I know, Raphael, but I don't want you to hurt."

He smiled and slid a curl away from my face. "I have you by my side. That hurt is nothing compared to the gift you give me every day."

I covered his hand with my own and smiled. "The same as you give me. Now I need to attend to my hair and—"

"I'll wait right here." He moved to the chair beside a dressing screen as I hurried to the bathroom.

* * *

The *Lady Anthea* made short work of our journey. By sunset, the dirigible was dropping through the clouds. I held on to the rails and watched our descent, my hair billowing free of the pins.

"Come inside, my fire."

I turned and looked at him with a smile.

Shouts echoed, and I spun toward the noise. A plume of black smoke rose near the gate of Nobel Crest.

Raphael lurched out, holding on to the railing and leaning forward. "What's going on?"

The closer we dropped, the clearer it became. Fierce fighting was taking place below, and to the side, a figure darted to a boat. "Is that...?"

"Edward? It appears so." Raphael's hands curled on the wood. "Bastard. Escaping before we can enact justice. Coward."

I slid my hand over Raphael's. It tensed, then relaxed. "Won't the others...?"

"That's a Casa Bonita boat. Fast. We're not equipped at this time to chase him."

I heard his disappointment.

"Even so, Nobel Crest is deregistered. I mean, Bloom can transfer the ownership to you still, right? Without Edward there?"

Raphael nodded. "Yes."

"So we go in there, we release the women, and we work out a plan where Nobel Crest as a property survives without the need of unwilling brides and more children than a normal man should have. Where everyone is equal." Tears pricked my eyes. "We'll do right by them, won't we?"

Raphael turned to me and smiled. "We'll make Nobel Crest a better place. Somewhere to be proud of. Maybe it can become a part of the Whitmore Foundation."

"The Nobel-Whitmore Foundation. Damien and Ammy both agreed the names belong together."

His smile grew large. "That sounds about right, Dr Nobel."

"And maybe we can give our child a legacy of kindness."

"Child?" His brow quirked.

"Well, I'm not sure, but..." I grinned. "Wait and see, my husband. Wait and see."

The End...
For Now.

***Did you enjoy this book by Imogene Nix?
There's more on the following pages. Just keep turning to see what else.***

When Cupid—otherwise known as Diocail— is banished from his home on a remote Scottish Island, he's set a series of tasks by the great god Lugh, who also happens to be his father.

In **Blame The Wine**, he must bring two lovers together... BBW Cara and James, the man she's lusted over from afar who happens to be a super geek and head Veha Industries.

In **A Stranger's Embrace**, Diocail is driven to help an emotionally fragile Jane and Davis, a famous author. The task is more complicated, with the existence of Carstairs her could-be ex-husband and teenage daughter, Frannie.

In **Revenge on Cupid**, Diocail must take the ultimate chance and find his own happily ever after with Simone. Sometimes the past gets in the way and HEA's don't come cheap though.

The dusty, dingy little diner was full, even with its current state of cleanliness—or lack thereof. People from the surrounding offices didn't care about anything except the incredible, well-prepared food at a reasonable cost. They flooded in, like waves to the shore. As one tide left, another swept in.

"Honestly, Simone. I'm going to try getting his attention one more time. If that doesn't work, I'm out of there. I mean, how long can I keep trying?" Cara picked at the caramel tart she hadn't been able to resist with the cheap metal fork and flicked the blob of fresh cream that sat on top to the side of the plate.

"You've said that tons of times before. Besides, what are you going to do to get his attention? Hmm? Walk naked through the typing pool?" Simone bobbed the straw in her smoothie as she eyed her friend with a frown. "It's been what? Eighteen months since you saw him, and you've mooned over him from a distance ever since you met him. You need to move on, Cara. That is, unless there's something you haven't shared?"

The query was arch. Cara shivered even as she shook her head. "No."

Simone quirked an eyebrow, obviously unconvinced with the answer. Cara let out a deep sigh of frustration. "There's a position...it's only temporary, for a PA reporting directly to him." She speared a forkful of tart, chewed quickly and swallowed, before continuing. "In his office, full-time for the period of the engagement. I saw the memo yesterday. I mean, I have the skills, right? I can type, answer phones, make coffee, file, greet people. What's more, I can probably do it better than all those size eights in the typing pool that Ms. Jackman seems to prefer." She nodded thoughtfully. "All I have to do is get past the ogre in Human Resources."

Simone stared at her, disbelief clear on her face. "Girl, I so remember that woman. If you think you can get past her, you're doing better than I ever did. That's why I left Veha Industries, remember? Maybe it's time to haul out your resumé and consider some other options. Look for something better." Simone shook her head and billows of her crimson hair swirled through the still air.

Cara understood Simone only had her best interests at heart. But this time she knew the outcome would be different. Hell, she could feel it in the air. The tingle of expectation.

"Cara, the HR ogre will hang you out for breakfast before she offers you anything like a position in that office. Remember her mantra? Good looks and good work make for a positive workplace!"

Simone didn't sugar-coat anything. It was another great reason for their long- term friendship. Honesty. But Cara didn't want to hear the truth in the statement. Even if it was exactly as her friend said.

Cara nodded quickly. "Yeah, I know, but if I don't try, then I won't know how close I can get to him, right? And the only way to catch his attention is to get past *her* and see him in person." Cara quaked a little at the information she needed to share. The favor she needed to ask. "Anyway, I tidied up my resumé and dropped the application into a memo envelope yesterday, so it's too late to back out now. I mean, fortune favors the brave. Doesn't it? If I don't snag an interview, I'm going to visit the career advisor across the street and register with them." She shrugged. "I'll look for temp work until something more long-term shows up. I can see what they have on offer and well...who knows? Maybe a job with the right boss is just waiting for me. But I'd rather this worked out, to be honest." Her voice trailed off into a whisper. "I really wish he would notice me."

Simone took a long slurp of her banana drink, and Cara noticed her questioning gaze even as she squirmed. Finally, Simone nodded. "It's your funeral. So anyway, you'd better show me this memo if you want me to be a referee for you. I'm guessing that's what you need, right? I'll have to know what I'm supposed to say about you before they ring."

Cara smiled. "Thanks, Simone. I knew I could count on you." She slipped a piece of paper out of her handbag and handed it over. "Sorry it's a bit creased. It was in the bottom of my bag, I stashed it so none of the others from the pool would see. You know how it is."

Available from Love Books Publishing
books2read.com/CelticCupid

Direct Autographed Copy
https://www.imogenenix.net/CelticCupid

Star of Ishtar

Warriors of the Elector
Book One

The first time Elara laid eyes on Grayson was when he rescued her from the clutches of a madman and his scientists who were kidnapping humans and conducting horrific experiments on them. That was years ago. In spite of her attempts to deepen their relationship, they remained nothing more than close friends. Now Elara is a medic with the Admiralty, and she knows what she wants. It's been Grayson since the beginning. When Elara is stationed on the *Star of Ishtar*, she arrives with a plan to further her career. But this time her plan has an added bonus—to finally get her man.

Grayson's spent years fighting the connection between himself and Elara. He's certain it only exist because he saved her life. But his will is failing, and he fears he just might give in to temptation.

"I finally made it." Elara Sudonne watched as the hull of the *Star of Ishtar* loomed in the inky darkness. She clutched her hands tightly together as the shuttle approached the hulking battleship.

This would be her new home and first combat ST placement for the Earth Empire. She quaked inwardly with nerves but fought to keep her serene exterior. Previously her deployments had consisted solely of on-planet expeditions and in rehabilitation and dirtside facilities. When the chance had arisen to move to the battleship, she'd grabbed it with both hands.

The frigid air chilled her bones as she sat in her shuttle seat, but a trickle of sweat inched its way down her back under the fresh gray wool flight uniform. Little puffs of vapor escaped her mouth as she rubbed her arms. Nerves stretched tight, she looked through the small portal at the front of the vessel. She wanted to tug at the collar that somehow seemed to have grown tighter as the ship loomed ahead, but instead she firmed her mouth, straightened her spine, and concentrated on the future.

"So damned long." She'd been working toward this outcome since the day Grayson Myatt and Duvall McCord had saved her from her Ru'Edan captors. She was lucky, she'd survived the 'experimentation' of the Ru'Edan leader Crick Sur Banden's scientists. "And all I have to remind me are my scars." She didn't grin at her own joke.

The person seated behind her jostled but she ignored it, lost in her memories. On that day, so very long ago, the young Elara, fresh-faced and with idealistic views of the empire, was taken from the mall where she'd been shopping with friends, thrust into the back of a transport vehicle, and given to the Ru'Edan scientists to experiment on.

For days they'd worked on her and others, seeking an average pain threshold of humans, slicing her skin then noting reactions and how long it took to heal. They'd cut her arms, body, and even her face, and now she carried the extensive scarring of the exercise as a reminder to herself and others of what they were fighting for. Freedom. The freedom of Earth and its allied planets.

She'd never relinquished hope, it had been her constant companion as she fought against the all-consuming terror. Then they'd found her in that dirty, disused warehouse. They'd found others too, in various states of death and decay. The smells of despair had filled the air with a fetid ripeness that she'd never been able to forget.

Since that day she'd promised herself that she would pay the Ru'Edan back for what they'd done to her. What they'd taken from her. Over the years, she tempered and honed the rage while remaining adamant that she would see the final act played out. She couldn't physically fight, but she had learned about trauma, knew it and understood how it affected a person, and used it as a weapon.

The iron will forged through her experiences had fed her determination, and she'd applied herself to study, finishing in the top ten percent of her class. She entered the medical program at the academy, working hard to excel. Her family remained supportive if perplexed as to why she had chosen to keep reminding herself of what had happened.

The maw of the *Star of Ishtar* loomed closer, opening its cavernous mouth as she watched through the portal. She could hear the voices of the shuttle crew signaling their intention to enter and land, the tinny confirmation coming swiftly. She watched avidly while the shuttle maneuvered, imagining the invisible shields dropping to allow it entry.

Her hands twisted with fear and anger, but she tamped down her emotions. Anger never helped anyone. Staying strong, knowing your history, and ensuring it couldn't be repeated, they were the answers, she told herself firmly, pulling herself from the grip of a dark past so horrific she still saw it in her dreams. She pushed it away to the recesses of her mind and focused on what she was about to do.

A squark overhead, the usual mechanical sound that alerted all on board to a transmission by the captain, caught her attention. "Attention all passengers. We are entering the shuttle bay. Please ensure when you disembark you remove all personal items. Move beyond the white line and wait for your designation."

The lights of the bay flashed as they entered, and once again Elara marveled at how far humanity had moved since they had first walked the Earth. She saw the opening of the structure as the shuttle moved into the bay, inching forward slowly until it stopped its ponderous motion and began its descent to the floor. Something deep inside warmed even as the shuttle's environmental systems began to synchronize with the cooler temperature of the *Star of Ishtar*, and she felt a smile crawl its way over her face.

Elara breathed in deeply, inhaling the metallic-tasting, recycled air and welcoming the calmness that settled on her body. Her eyes closed as she filled her lungs. "I'm here." There was more than a little satisfaction in her tone, and she smiled. She slowly exhaled, finding that center of peace she relied on.

A loud thud and clank echoed as the deep drone split the air. The engines were powering down, and there she was, on one of the Earth Empire's Emeritus class battleships. She sat in her seat, waiting for the all clear from the captain, and once it sounded through the cabin, she rose, tugging at the webbing belt and disengaging it.

The small backpack beside her was all she carried as she made her way to the exit, not needing to duck as so many others did. She stepped through the door, her hands gripping the rail of the cold, metal stairs which connected to the side of the gray shuttle.

She clambered down them slowly, savoring the experience. The sting of the cold on her hands from the stairs, frigid from even their brief exposure to the blackness of space, made her flinch inwardly. The shuttle journey from the Admiralty's strategic base at Aenna to their current position had taken just over an hour, but the whole time it felt like her heart had been in her throat. Her mouth was dry as she followed the new recruits from the ship into the landing bay. She stopped, silently noting the slight mustiness of the air, the recycled quality easily recognizable. Everything, including the oxygen, needed recycling in space.

All around her people swarmed, either around the ships or into the dogleg line that now formed ahead of her. Someone had opened the baggage locker of the shuttle, and the sound of dropping bags hitting the plascrete floor echoed in the air. Another crewmember guided trolleys to the other side of the shuttle, pulling out boxes with important day-to-day items for the ship, including vaccines and plants. She watched briefly, all the while listening to the alien cacophony. Voices called in welcome to old crewmembers, while new ones watched, many goggle-eyed in the fresh uniforms of newly minted officers and crewmembers.

Her gaze flicked around quickly, taking in the sights, sounds, and smells, pungent with oils and grease; burning smells from the scorched plascrete and the press of sweaty or nervous bodies. She joined the line silently, tacking onto the end, and stayed at parade rest, knowing the welcoming voice would cut through the air soon enough. She felt somehow disconnected from the main throng. Perhaps the knowledge that this was the outcome she had worked for years to achieve set her apart. However, still, she felt so...distant from everything around her. She smiled secretly at the bout of whimsy.

"Attention!" The voice boomed out over the plascrete of the docking bay, and she snapped her body into position, noting the commander who had bellowed the words. Technically, she outranked most members aboard the *Star of Ishtar*, except for the command and leadership staff, but she knew all newcomers had to join the welcoming parade, regardless of rank.

Fleet Captain Elphin came into view, his tired features topped by salt-and-pepper gray hair, which highlighted his cool blue eyes. Elara also recognized a body prone to a little middle-aged thickness. Following behind him was his second-in-command, Duvall McCord. A young up-and-coming officer, his status as a fast-tracking officer heading toward his own command, with Elphin both his mentor and captain, had become almost legendary at the academy.

She looked closely at McCord, noting the dynamic drive of his actions and movements. Soon he would achieve a promotion to captain, and she rejoiced for her friend. She'd followed his career with interest and had to tamp down a smile as his eyes betrayed the shock of seeing her before settling into their flat command persona. So he hadn't been apprised of her deployment, she noted, and she had to restrain the tiny feeling of surprise and satisfaction. She filed that snippet of information away.

She caught sight of the man standing behind Duvall. Grayson Myatt. He'd made her heart beat faster for years. Tall and blond with a muscular build and a sexy, tight, little butt, he had pools of deep-blue eyes that had always made her think of forever. He had a growth of stubble on his chiseled jaw, and her fingers itched to touch his perfect lips. Yes, since the day he'd found her in that nasty warehouse tied down like a ragged animal, she'd worshipped him from afar.

Now she had her opportunity to tangle with him, hopefully much closer than any chance that had ever come her way before. With a sigh, she pulled her gaze back to the captain and forced herself to concentrate on his words. She couldn't afford to have her commanding officer angry due to her being distracted.

"Welcome to the *Star of Ishtar*. Most academy recruits want to join us because of what we represent, but on this ship, we only take the best of the best. So, if you made it here, you're the ones we wanted to take a look at. Getting here is only the first step. Staying here is harder to achieve. Our people are the best. Earn your place, and in return, we'll make you one of our crew—a member of the *Star of Ishtar*. Only the best and the brightest wear our uniform and badge. You'll be expected to perform to your absolute limit then give some more. We don't tolerate people who don't pull their weight. Do us proud and wear your uniform with pride." The captain looked out over the new members of his crew. His voice had echoed during his speech, and now it died away.

He scanned the faces before him, and she could almost read his thoughts. There were new security officers and a smattering of other crew. Some of them were young and impressionable, and she knew a few wouldn't make the cut as crewmembers. Others would carve out their place on the *Star of Ishtar* and move to better positions and placements, like she would: the new SurgiTech, a younger female, experienced but untried on board a ship. She smiled at that thought.

Some of those who stood with her would be replaced as they failed the exacting standards the captain set. She'd heard that he was a firm captain, fair but demanding. He'd have to be to command this ship. The

Ishtar had well over five hundred at full capacity, and the captain could select their placements as his command staff saw fit from the many who applied to join the crew. She sensed his satisfaction with the choices in the relaxation of his body.

Abruptly, he turned to Duvall, breaking her study of him. "Get them to where they need to present themselves." His words echoed as he walked away. He had a purposeful stride. Quick but unhurried, like he knew where he was going and how to get there. A man who knew how to get what he wanted. Someone to respect and admire.

"My name is Commander Duvall McCord. I am your second-in-command, and my direct subordinate is Commander Grayson Myatt. While you are aboard the *Star of Ishtar* you will be required to fulfill your duties efficiently. As Captain Elphin said, do your job right and you will be one of ours, with all the benefits that come with being a crewmember of the *Star of Ishtar*."

He paused and eyeballed each of the newer recruits, those fresh from the academy. Many of them paled under his gaze, and she smiled inwardly. Even the older people in the line seemed to quake beneath his scowl. He'd always had that air of innate authority, even when barely out of the academy himself. She knew his methods and watched him make full use of the carefully practiced tone of presence.

"Each of you has been assigned. You will present yourselves to the chief of your section. Those details will be found in your orders. Commander Myatt has organized a team to escort you to your cabins. You will have approximately one hour to prepare. We've arranged for crewmembers to escort you to your superiors. Be ready to present for duty. Any issues, you will, of course, take up with your section commander. Should there be need to take any further action, you will see Commander Myatt. You should only see me if you are a command crewmember or as a point of discipline. I am not one for small talk, so if you present to me, have a very good reason."

He delivered the words slowly and deliberately, and Elara restrained a small smile on hearing at least one gulp from those in the line nearest her.

"We run a tight ship here. Discipline and commitment are the two key factors we look for beyond loyalty in our crew. You will from henceforth represent our ship everywhere, and we do not tolerate anything less than the best." He looked around once more, the stern demeanor he wore so well reinforcing the message. If she hadn't known him for so long, she too might have missed the hint of humor glinting in his eyes, the one many took for coldness.

Her legs ached, and she wanted to move and relieve the pressure on them, but she held herself still, waiting for the command to dismiss. She wouldn't let herself or him down now. Not after she'd worked so long to achieve this position.

As the new ST, she had no previous experience on ships. She had vast experience in the field, but Elara was aware that would count for little in the eyes of most of the crew. She didn't intend to signal a weakness to anyone and least of all on her first day aboard the *Star of Ishtar*. That thought held her still and controlled.

She had big shoes to fill after her predecessor, Jamieson, had retired, even though she knew she could fill the void he'd left behind. As a long-term member of the crew—over twenty years—his tenure on the *Star of Ishtar* had placed him aboard since its launch. Due to his experience in the heat of battle with the Ru'Edan he had made a name for himself as the coldest of cold in the hottest of situations. She hoped to emulate that herself and carve out her own place aboard the Ishtar, as its crew lovingly knew her.

Duvall and Grayson knew how much she wanted to prove herself. They just wouldn't have expected it here, on the Ishtar.

She watched Duvall study her, then, quickly turning on his heel, call to those assembled, "Dismissed."

Once they started to move away, she softened her stance, preparing to turn when the call came.

"Sudonne! A moment if you please."

Elara turned to face Duvall. "Commander?"

"Welcome to the *Star of Ishtar*, Elara. While I am surprised you're the new ST, Grayson and I are pleased you could join us. But how did you manage to pull it off? Keeping it quiet that you were the new ST?" he asked, his voice deep enough to make most women shiver with anticipation.

She smiled, thinking it was a shame she didn't have any feelings for him except sisterly attachment, but then again, given his lack of deep commitment to women, maybe it wasn't such a shame after all.

She understood what drove him. He wanted his own ship and to captain his own future. They'd spent many nights over wine or ale discussing his beliefs that commitment grounded a person. Inwardly, she shrugged. He'd make those calls for himself, though she was sure that one day he would come across someone who would make him consider his choices a little more thoroughly.

"I'm pleased to be here, Duvall. Having an uncle who happens to be an admiral, he was able to let Captain Elphin know that I wanted to surprise you. It's a small world in the Admiralty. Elphin already knew of me, so he okayed my placement. Once the powers knew there was no impediments to me joining the crew, it was fairly simple from there." She felt a small smile creep onto her face, then let it drop away. "What do you think Grayson thinks?"

"Ah, still chasing him, are you?" He grinned, his eyes twinkling. "I think he'll be pleased you're finally old enough and you're here." He looked her straight in the eye. "But you may just need to remind him of that particular fact." He motioned for her to go before him, barking out a deep laugh. "Come on, I'll show you to your cabin."

Available from Love Books Publishing
Available in Ebook via Books2Read

Direct Autographed Copy
https://www.imogenenix.net/Warriors1

The Blood Bride by Imogene Nix

Hope just wants to be an ordinary nestling. She went to college and escaped, but now she's back and there's a secret everyone is keeping from her.

Xavier is the new master of the nest, ready to welcome home the daughter of the house who he has never met. He's unprepared for the woman who steals his breath and enchants him.

Now Hope and Xavier must fight for lives and those of the innocents. After all, it is only by overcoming the rogues that they will have a chance of a timeless future together. But will it be in time?

* * *

PROLOGUE

As silence descended on the house, the shadows grew—dark grays and blacks that bled into each other. First one figure then another broke away, making a run toward the house. Silent as the grave, they moved swiftly over dew-slicked grass. Then they stopped still. Waiting. Not a movement betrayed them until a signal propelled them back into action and they started crawling upwards. The walls damp coating no barrier to the intruders that ascended in the darkness.

The sound of each window breaking shattered the quiet—the figures were inside. Screams echoed through the night. Yet, in this area of large estates, heavy with noise-absorbing shrubbery, no one could hear those within. The blood-curdling screams went on and on before finally dying away.

Just one sound echoed through the night: The sobbing of a child.

The front door opened and figures trooped out—ghostly specters against an inky night sky, broken by a single outline. A child in white, carried at the center of the pack.

No sound broke the silence as they moved toward the trees surrounded the house.

Flames now licked at the manor: A deathly glow of oily smoke rising.

All that remained was a single person—wrapped in a cape of midnight blue beyond the house—watching them melt away.

Jemima moved toward the burning structure, breaking into a run as she breached the threshold. Vainly she attempted to enter, but the heat drove her back.

Now dashing tears from her face, she raced across the graveled driveway toward the gates, where the guardhouse was located. No sign of life existed within the building and some instinct of survival slowed her pace to a careful creep. Out of breath and heaving from exertion, she nervously checked within.

Small puffs of white vapor colored the glass. She darted from one window to another. Her cloak drawn tightly around her body, hoping it would camouflage her from sight.

Satisfied, Jemima entered through the heavy, wooden front door and moved toward the phone she spied on the floor. Her eyes darting here and there she dialed, listening to the rotary motor as it returned to the proper position. Time was short and if *they* came back, she needed to have shared the message.

The phone rang once. Twice. With a brrping sound it connected.

"Hello?" A male answered and she felt a warm flush of relief at the voice. A voice she knew well.

"The manor has been breached. The girl child taken." The words erupted and her hand trembled.

"On our way." The click of the receiver being replaced echoed loudly in the stillness of the room.

Copper. She smelled copper.

Her stomach soured, knowing it meant more deaths. Jemima looked around for the gun—a gun with deadly, holy water-infused copper bullets—she knew was hidden somewhere in the room. A gun she couldn't find. *No divine intervention exists here*, she thought.

Hopefully *they* didn't remain. Feeding. If they were still here, that's what they would be doing. She found a corner and scrunched down, hiding from sight.

Crouched low, she tried to stay as still as possible, listening for sounds of the vehicles she knew would be coming. She dug her fingers into the flesh of her arms; remaining aware enough to stop before drawing blood. That would surely bring them out. Jemima dragged the cloak around her to capture the warmth, yet there was little to be found.

The sounds of engines roused her from the corner of the room. Jemima inched toward the window, the lead of the old glass distorting her view, hearing raised voices she knew Mistress Cressida had arrived.

Jemima retreated. Remained hidden from the woman because if she knew, all may well be lost. From the shadowed room she listened to the conversation...

"It smells like Estersham." The Mistress' eyes closed. "If it is, we have a problem." She turned once more, her face set and eyes now glacial in intensity. "James?"

The man nodded as if he knew what was to come.

"If I take those steps, I cannot return. Another must stand in my place." Her voice hardened while her eyes glittered in the dim light, piercing in their intensity.

Then the Mistress' voice called out in the near silence. "You and yours have been my loyal servants for so many years. I took an oath to protect you long ago. I renewed it with marriage and births, over and over. Now, my home and yours have been breached and this child taken from us. The girl child, who will be the hope and salvation of our kind, was ripped from the bosom of our nest. I will repay your loyalty and I will get her back." The words of power rippled in the night and licked at Jemima's skin.

Available in Ebook
books2read.com/BloodBride-Nix

Direct Autographed Copy
https://www.imogenenix.net/BloodBride

Also by Imogene Nix

<u>**Warriors of the Elector**</u>

- Star of Ishtar
- Starline
- Starfire
- Star of the Fleet
- Starburst
- The Star of Eternity

The Star of Ishtar & Starline - Print

Starfire & Star of the Fleet - Print

Starburst & The Star of Eternity - Print

<u>**Blood Secrets**</u>

- The Blood Bride
- The Illuminated Witch
- The Sorcerer's Touch

<u>*The Secrets World:*</u>

<u>**Blood Secrets**</u>

- The Blood Bride
- The Illuminated Witch
- The Sorcerer's Touch

<u>**House Secrets**</u>

- As Dawn Breaks
- Immortal Consequences
- Unnamed Book III

All That Glitters - a House Secrets Novella (Coming in 2023)

Danu's Secrets

- The Downfall of Padraic O'Shaunessy (Coming in 2023)
- Unnamed Secrets Book II

The Automaton Series

- Haven House
- Nobel Crest

The Search Duology

- Miss Elspeth's Desire
- Miss Isabelle's Craving

Duology World Novels

- A Very Merry Widow (coming soon)

Reunion Trilogy

- War's End
- The Assassin
- Executing Justice

The Reunion Trilogy in Paperback

Sex Love & Aliens

- Tangled Webs
- False Webs
- Covert Webs

21st Testing Protocol

- Cyborg: Redux

- Children Of A Greater Evil
- When Evil Came To Stay
- Finis: The War To End All Wars

Celtic Cupid Trilogy

- Blame The Wine
- A Stranger's Embrace
- Revenge On Cupid

The Celtic Cupid Trilogy in Paperback

Zombieology

- The Reset
- I Dream of Zombies
- The Six Million Dollar Zombie
- Make Room For Zombies
- Days of Our Zombies (coming 2023)
- Unnamed Zobiology title (coming soon)

Knights of Pleasure

- Silken Knights (Coming in 2022)

Single Titles

The Chocolate Affair (also in Print)

Falling In Love Again (Previously A Sapphire For Karina)

BioCybe (also in Print)

Hesparia's Tears (also in Print)

Tomorrow's Promise

A Bar In Paris (also in Print)

Inheritance Of The Blood (also in Print)

The Plan

Loving Memories (also in Print)

Hero of Heartbreak Hill (also in Print)

My One & Only

Curse Bound (coming 2021)

Raspberry Dreams (Not Yet Released)

Non Fiction

Self Publishing: Absolute Beginners Guide (With Suzi Love)

Written as Ciara Cave

25 Curated Ways To Get Rid Of Telemarketers

Book Signings for Absolute Beginners

About the Author

Imogene is published in a range of romance genres including Paranormal, Science Fiction and Contemporary. She is mainly published in the UK and USA.

In 2010, Imogene Nix (the pen name not Imogene herself) was born. Imogene sat down and worked tirelessly for 3 months culminating in the book Starline, which became the first in a trilogy titled, "Warriors of the Elector." Since then she's had over 30 titles published and is now focusing on hybridising herself - with a mixture of traditionally published and self-published works.

In fact, she's taking control of many of her back catalogue books, which are slowly re-releasing as self-published titles.

Imogene is a member of a range of professional organisations world wide, and believes in the mantra of mentoring and paying it forward and is actively involved in mentorship (through NaNoWrimo and her vlog: In The Chair With Imogene Nix) and tutoring of new and upcoming authors.

In her spare time she loves to drink coffee, wine & eat chocolate and is parenting her spoiled dog and a ferocious cat along with her husband and daughter and looks forward to weekends away with her husband in their caravan "The Seven Year Hitch!" Do look forward to her caravan romance at some point!

To Contact Imogene
www.imogenenix.net
imogene@imogenenix.net

Sign up for her newsletter at
https://www.imogenenix.net/Signup

facebook.com/ImogeneNix

twitter.com/ImogeneNix

instagram.com/ImogeneNix

bookbub.com/authors/imogenenix